All You Need is a Duke

The Duke Hunters Club, Volume 1

Bianca Blythe

D1608144

Published by Bianca Blythe, 2020.

This is a work of fiction. Similarities to real people, places, or events are entirely coincidental.

ALL YOU NEED IS A DUKE

First edition. February 23, 2020.

Written by Bianca Blythe.

CHAPTER ONE

JUNE 1820
London

The first rule of being a wallflower was to acquire a superb seat.

Margaret Carberry, daughter of the Scottish tycoon of the same surname and relation of absolutely no aristocrats, was no longer a novice at attending balls: her mother accepted every invitation.

Margaret strode toward the quietest section of the ballroom, farthest removed from the musicians and dancers, just as she did at every ball. Juliet and Genevieve would be here, and she wove through the horde of partygoers with expertise. Women wore thin white gowns embellished with pastel ribbons and trimmed with lace, an obvious effort to counter the summer heat. Men flashed strained smiles, discernibly uncomfortable in their complexly tied cravats, jewel-colored waistcoats and snug tailcoats, the latter a product of a season of feasting.

The second rule of being a wallflower was to not interact with anyone. Margaret didn't need to see the expressions of the guests shift when they worried they might need to converse. Though the upper echelon didn't tend toward timidity, few desired to be seen speaking with her.

Matchmaking mamas and proud papas no longer pondered whether they should drag their second and third-born sons to meet her, and Margaret no longer felt awkward attempting to talk with the *ton*: after all, the results remained the same. The *crème de la crème* frowned at the first lilts of her Scottish accent, and when they ascertained the identity of her father, they hastily excused themselves. Even those in possession of imposing debts deemed it preferable to endure uneasy encounters with their tailors and slash their servant number than jeopardize their respectability.

The *ton* was suspicious of her presence at the occasional festivity, seeing it as indicative of an unnecessary downgrade of society, reminiscent of ideals that might be shared by the pitchfork-wielding peasants who once roamed the other side of the channel. Her father might be wealthier than many of them put together, she might have attended the same finishing school as other daughters of the *ton,* but that didn't mean she belonged.

Margaret would simply find a good seat, then chat with her dear friends. Even Mama wouldn't expect her to find a husband at the last ball of the season. Margaret smiled, even though when she'd first attended a ball, her lips had hurt from the effort of feigning delight. Now she almost enjoyed attending these evening engagements.

The throng thickened, and Margaret placed her hand on her turban to hinder any instincts the feathers on it might have to flutter away. The only thing worse than wearing a feathered monstrosity would be to wear a destroyed feathered monstrosity.

No matter.

This was the last event of the season: it was almost over.

Perhaps she hadn't found a husband, but she wouldn't be the first woman not betrothed after one season. Besides, Papa was hardly impoverished. Perhaps Mama would agree she didn't require a second season, and that she could simply find a cottage in Dorset and live blissfully ensconced with her favorite science tomes.

Violins hummed pleasantly. Margaret's body lightened, and she quickened her gait.

Suddenly, something wet cascaded down her dress, and a definite alcoholic scent invaded her nostrils. She furrowed her brow, but she hadn't imagined it—icy liquid cascaded down her back.

Fiddlesticks.

A champagne flute shattered below her feet on the Duke of Jevington's polished pine floorboards, marring the elaborate chalk design, and Margaret bit back a scream. What had she done? Evidently, Margaret's newfound experience at balls had not prepared her for avoiding toppling glassware. Liquid seeped over Margaret's gown.

Double fiddlesticks.

She patted her back tentatively and dropped her gaze to the broken shards of glass, imprinted with an elaborate gold design.

Well, the design was currently less elaborate.

A few matrons shot Margaret horrified glances, widening their mouths and furrowing their brows, in uncharacteristic disregard for the potential formation of wrinkles.

A footman hastened toward her, clutching a white handkerchief. He dove to the floor, gathering the glass shards.

Some debutantes angled their torsos toward the commotion and smirked. Their puffed sleeves remained unmarred by any sudden liquid contact, and their embroidered fabric exuded an alcoholic scent-free perfection.

Margaret's stomach twisted. This ball was supposed to be enjoyable. And she'd ruined it.

Someone grabbed Margaret's elbow, and when Margaret turned, she saw her mother.

"I saw what happened," Mama said briskly. "How clumsy of you. I marched straight over."

"I-I'm sorry," Margaret stammered, taken aback by her mother's abrupt appearance. "I don't know how—"

Mama waved her hand in an uncharacteristic lackadaisical manner. "It's of no importance, my dear."

Margaret's mouth dropped open. Most things were of absolute importance to Mama. Making a good impression on the Duke of Jevington certainly ranked at the top of Mama's desires. This was his ball, and he was unlikely to be enamored by the woman who'd transformed his glossy polished floor into a danger zone.

Not that the duke would be enamored even if Margaret hadn't somehow accidentally toppled a glass of champagne. Even other wallflowers deemed Margaret dull. No duke desired to have a duchess who stumbled when she spoke and whose cheeks reddened at short intervals. The fact Margaret was apt to speak about facts with the same enthusiasm as others rhapsodized about lofty acquaintances was little solace.

"You must get dry." Mama linked arms with Margaret, as if wary Margaret might desire to scamper toward the other dancers in her dripping attire to attempt a reel.

They inched toward the exit as more people swarmed into the ballroom. Some people regarded Margaret curiously, perhaps wondering why Margaret had decided that pleasant music, dancing and food were experiences to be abandoned, rather than savored. Others were occupied with craning their necks toward the wonders of the painted ceiling, complete with cherubs and cerulean skies, even if neither sight was frequent over Grosvenor Square.

Finally, Margaret and her mother moved past the sturdy carved wooden doors and onto the glossy black-and-white marble tiles of the duke's foyer. Margaret stepped toward the cloakroom. Leaving early was embarrassing, but at least they hadn't spotted the duke: that had to be a triumph. The moment seemed deficient in glory, but Margaret raised her chin anyway. More alcohol dripped down her back, and she shuddered.

Mama pulled Margaret's sleeve. "Let's go upstairs."

"Upstairs?" Margaret's voice trembled.

Guests didn't venture upstairs.

"B-But." Margaret halted. She felt ridiculous reminding her mother about societal rules. After all, her mother had taught them to her.

Mama giggled, even though Mama never giggled.

Margaret narrowed her eyes. Her mother was acting most oddly. She may have longed for her mother to be less strict and dogmatic, but she certainly hadn't expected Mama to transform into a woman who went about cavorting about the duke's townhouse.

"No need for you to be stodgy, dear," Mama said. "If I say, it's appropriate, it is."

Mama had always seemed to be the epitome of appropriateness before.

Margaret hesitated, but her mother yanked her toward an imposing staircase. Coldness not merely attributed to the champagne spillage slinked along Margaret's spine.

"We mustn't go there," Margaret said. "The duke's accommodations are there."

"Nonsense," Mama whispered. "You cannot have champagne on your dress. It's unseemly. Besides, the duke is in the ballroom."

Mama's eyes sparkled, and her lips remained curved in a manner more commonly found in people attending comic operas. She proceeded purposefully up the marble stairs, sweeping the hem of her dress against the balustrade with such force that some of the bows on the hem of her gown unraveled. Clearly, Mama's lady's maid had not prepared for Mama's energy.

Margaret shuddered at what Mama might do upstairs, where she might indulge in any snooping tendencies. Mama could hardly wander alone in the private corners of the townhouse.

Margaret glanced in the butler's direction. Thankfully, he was consumed with guarding the door—not the things that happened inside the townhouse. Margaret sighed and followed her mother, sliding a laced glove hand over the banister. Gilt-framed paintings of various lovely landscapes, presumably of the Duke's extensive properties, lined the stairs. Everything was beautiful, even if art enthusiasts were unlikely to clamber up the steps to scrutinize the paintings. Whatever other paintings were in the townhouse would be even more special.

The unlit landing seemed foreboding, but a maid soon approached them at the landing, clasping a lantern. Margaret shrank back. They'd been discovered.

Fiddle-faddle.

Margaret shifted her legs, preparing herself for an icy stare and a firm word, the sort Margaret's classmates had received at their finishing school, but which had never been directed at her. Margaret obeyed rules, even the unwritten ones. She knew better than to wander upstairs, even if the duke was not currently roaming the darkened corridors.

This was when the maid would tell them to leave. Instead, the maid nodded at Mama. "This way."

Margaret blinked. Had the maid witnessed the incident and ascended another staircase? But maids were generally not present at balls. Perhaps a footman had informed her? Margaret furrowed her brow.

The maid strode briskly, marching past sideboards and oversized blue-and-white porcelain vases that looked lavish even in the poor light, and Mama and Margaret hurried after her. Their feet sank into luxurious carpets that muffled their steps, but the odd silence didn't soothe Margaret's ever-faster beating heart. A beatific smile radiated on Mama's lips, even though normally she might grumble that the maid's speedy gait was unnecessary.

Finally, the maid halted before a door. "This is it."

"Thank you." Mama pressed something into the maid's hands. "I'm afraid I'll need your help."

The maid nodded gravely. "Of course. She's quite large."

In the next moment, the maid clasped hold of Margaret's wrists and dragged her inside the room.

"What are you doing?" Margaret blurted, struggling against the maid's sturdy clasp.

Confusion coursed through Margaret. Maids weren't supposed to pull one into rooms. *No one* was supposed to do that.

"Mama?" Margaret pleaded.

Fingers shoved Margaret. Fingers that did *not* belong to the maid. Both the maid's hands were clasped about Margaret's wrists, like makeshift handcuffs. The lavender scent her mother favored floated about Margaret in unmistakable fashion: Mama was forcing her into the room. Mama wasn't even prone to giving hugs, yet now she shoved Margaret's back.

"The bed's to the right," the maid said in a professional manner, as if she were explaining the room's layout to a new guest who'd entered the proper way, with an invitation.

"Please release me," Margaret said in her most authoritative tone. "What on earth is happening?"

"I'm ensuring your future peace and happiness," Mama squealed. "Isn't that wonderful?"

Margaret's heart plummeted.

An idea occurred to her.

An abominable, atrocious and alarming idea.

"Whose room is this?" Margaret's voice wobbled, struggling against a suddenly dry throat, as if she'd entered the Sahara, and not an opulent room in rainy, damp England.

"The Duke of Jevington's," Mama declared. "Your future husband."

Heavens.

Margaret squeezed her eyes shut. Unfortunately, when she opened them, the world remained the same as before.

"You're jesting," Margaret said. "You must be jesting."

Perhaps Mama had never jested before, and perhaps she'd involved this strange maid to assist in her joke, but that didn't mean she *wasn't* jesting.

Surely not.

Mama's wasn't actually going to stage a compromising situation, was she?

"The duke may have invited me to this townhouse, but that doesn't mean he desires me to be installed on his bed," Margaret said.

Mama laughed and pulled the door shut. The maid set the lantern on a table with a clank. Golden light illuminated a coffered ceiling. The air smelled of cedar and citrus, a masculine scent that differed from Margaret's own lavender smelling room.

A rosette fell from her dress onto the expensive-appearing rug below. Not that the duke would know its expense. Margaret's father made money, but a nobleman maintained his, and nobody was nobler than the Duke of Jevington. His ancestors had probably had the rug hauled from the Ottoman Empire during the Crusades, brought over the Alps with donkeys.

Fiddlesticks.

Some women's hearts might quicken at the thought of being the Duke of Jevington's wife. Unlike most dukes, he was of a marriageable age; though unlike most dukes, he was unmarried.

No doubt, Mama desired to change that particular fact.

The duke's handsomeness was renowned, filling potential grandmothers with happy thoughts of symmetrical faced babies when they weren't thinking of the man's vast estates and convenient coffers of money. The duke had managed to remain uncaught, despite having a town house in Mayfair, giving him easy access to matchmaking mamas and their desperate debutante daughters.

Besides, the Duke of Jevington wasn't going to permit himself to be compromised by anyone. She'd met him before: he was the best friend of her friend Lady Metcalfe's husband. She'd spent two highly uncomfortable weeks in the duke's presence at a house party. Not that they'd even had a conversation, but surely, if the duke were for some odd reason to declare a passion for her, he would have had an ample opportunity to do so then.

He'd probably relish the scandal even if Margaret's mother ushered the entire ballroom of guests to gawk at Margaret on the bed. It was the sort of thing that might gain a man a high position in the coveted *Rogues to Adore* list *Matchmaking for Wallflowers* released each year.

Margaret pulled against the maid's grip, but it had not lost its firmness.

The maid sneered, but Margaret resisted the urge to cry.

It would be fine.

It has to be.

She would convince her mother and the maid to release her, pick up her rosette from the floor, and if the duke noticed a scent of champagne when he entered the room tonight, he would merely attribute it to a pleasant memory of the festivity.

Margaret wasn't going to allow herself to become the laughingstock of the *ton*.

Not *again*.

Margaret raised her chin. "I demand to leave."

Mama stared for a moment. Her eyebrows and lower lip leaped in opposite directions, as if they desired to part.

Margaret refused to quiver.

Then Mama gave a youthful giggle. "You're not going to demand anything." She turned to the maid. "Where are the constraints?"

Constraints?

Margaret's eyebrows jerked up.

The maid pulled a long ribbon from her apron pocket. The ribbon looked appallingly sturdy, and Margaret pulled away. Her mother tightened her grip on Margaret.

"You can't tie me up," Margaret said quickly. "Besides, no one will believe he compromised me. The plan won't work."

The maid smirked. Most likely she was fully aware of the nonsensicalness of the plan. Just how much money had Mama promised her?

"My sweet child," Mama said. "I am very happy your innocence remains intact, but I assure you, people will believe you've been compromised if they discover you tied up."

Mama forced Margaret onto the four-poster bed and sat on her legs. Margaret writhed, but Mama was heavy, and the maid tied Margaret's wrists to each bedpost. Sapphire-colored panels swept down regally, swathing her in sumptuousness. The bed would be considered luxurious under most circumstances, but Margaret shivered as her skin pressed against the duke's blanket. She shouldn't be here. Doubtlessly more of the rosettes sewn onto her dress were toppling off.

"Shall I tie her ankles?" the maid asked.

"What?" Margaret wiggled on the bed, attempting to free herself.

"Don't say 'what,' dear," Mama said automatically. "I've been informed it's quite coarse. 'Excuse me' is far preferable. There is an addition of syllables, but politeness is always the goal."

"Courtesy is not my current concern," Margaret huffed.

A strand of her hair fell from her updo.

And then another one.

And then another one.

Margaret wished she were a pirate and had a large vocabulary of expletives to usher forth.

"When the duke returns to his room," Mama said. "He will find you."

"And he'll know he didn't put me here."

"It doesn't matter. You'll be discovered together. A witness will accompany me. I will be distraught." Mama clasped her hands together, and her lower lip trembled. She then beamed, as if triumphant at her acting abilities.

Margaret stared at her. "You've thought about this for some time."

"Daydreamed about it. And now, through some generous payments, it will be possible." Mama gave a grateful glance to the maid and clapped her hands. "Oh, think of the wedding we shall have for you. All of society will attend."

"Because they would not believe that the duke and I would ever wed."

"Your unpopularity will be a distant memory," Mama said, her voice brimming with confidence.

Margaret frowned.

Mama was being impossible. Ever since Papa had made them rich, Mama had wanted to marry Margaret off well. Unfortunately, it seemed easier for Papa to invent something and create a whole company from it than for Mama to snare a titled son-in-law. Obviously, Mama shouldn't be trying for dukes. Even the most experienced matchmaking mamas must waver at that goal.

"You'll lose your position if you do this," Margaret told the maid. "I'll tell the duke."

"Her future is safe," Mama said hastily, nodding at the maid. "Our townhouse can always sparkle more."

Margaret's mother opened her velvet brocade reticule and extracted a jar. Mama removed the lid and a pleasant floral scent wafted through the room.

"That scent will not calm me," Margaret said.

"Dearest, it's not your emotions I am concerned about."

Mama flitted through the room, moving from the canopied bed to the chaise-longue.

Her mother scattered something, humming.

Margaret widened her eyes. "Are you scattering rose petals?"

"I would think it would look obvious," Mama said. "All the better to make it romantic, my dear."

This was mad.

Margaret fought the temptation to scream. In all likelihood that would only lead her to have a gag placed in her mouth. Besides, this floor was empty, and the festivity had practically pulsated with noise.

Perhaps she could remove these clasps. It was unlikely, but right now, it was her only hope.

"You want her clothes on?" the maid asked.

"The answer is yes. Obviously," Margaret exclaimed.

"A tear will suffice," Mama said.

"Of course." The maid ripped the bodice of Margaret's gown efficiently.

"You don't have to do this, Mama," Margaret begged. "The plan won't work. Not that this is the way to marry me off. And we can just leave. No one will know. And I'll make more of an effort—I promise."

Mama scrunched her lips together, then strode toward Margaret.

Hope shot through Margaret.

Perhaps Mama really would free her. Perhaps everything would be fine.

Instead, Mama removed Margaret's pins from her hair. She removed a comb from her reticule and smoothed Margaret's hair.

Her eyes glimmered, and she pinched Margaret's cheeks. "Much better. You look most improper, like you've just been ravished.

Then Mama turned and exited the room with the maid.

Margaret was alone.

She'd known Mama had been eager to marry her off, but she hadn't realized she would resort to this. Shouldn't she have expected it? Hadn't Mama bribed someone to assist her when the Marquess of Metcalfe had openly searched for a wife?

Nausea tinged Margaret's throat.

If only Margaret had worked harder to find a husband this season. The next time someone even vaguely suitable showed any interest in her, Margaret vowed to marry him.

Most likely she wouldn't even have the chance to do that. Margaret would be ruined once she was discovered on the duke's bed.

Her heartbeat shook, and she surveyed her new surroundings.

Dark green fabric lined the walls, as if chosen to match the duke's hunting attire. Heavy furniture from past centuries dotted the room. Regal busts of Roman emperors perched on the tables. Clearly, the person who'd placed them there had not anticipated that women might be dragged into his room by their matchmaking mamas.

As beds went, this outranked others in sumptuousness. The pillow possessed a pleasant feather density, and the bed cords did not sag intolerably. The coverlet was suitably soft, and no wind wafted through the window. He had the proper number of pillows, and his bedding was appropriately soft. No doubt clouds could take advice from them.

But despite the silky texture, Margaret's heart still hammered, as if she were fleeing a criminal, and not lying on one of the most luxurious beds in Britain.

Margaret despised dancing, but she hardly desired to spend the duration of the ball here. She thought longingly of the rows of food on the banquet table. Genevieve and Juliet would probably wonder where she was.

At some point the Duke of Jevington would enter the room, and everything would be horrible.

Margaret continued to tug on her fastenings.

Unfortunately, they showed no signs of moving.

CHAPTER TWO

JASPER TIERNEY, THE Duke of Jevington, had never considered himself to excel at much of anything. His sporting abilities were tolerable, though he'd never seen the point of risking his neck to dive for a ball when playing rugby. His academic skills were worse. Harrow didn't include a course that bestowed good grades on a person's ability to make his classmates laugh, and Jasper lacked equal enthusiasm for declining Latin words and dividing fractions.

But Jasper had been wrong: he excelled at planning celebrations.

Jasper's parties were renowned, and he stood on the mezzanine as his guests danced and jested, drank and jubilated. Footmen carried silver platters in one hand, undaunted by the men and women who swarmed about them. Jovial music floated through the ballroom, and people swayed merrily, forming the familiar complex patterns with glee.

A year ago, Jasper would have joined them, but now observing sufficed. Party planning was exhausting, and his memory of the event would not be enhanced by a brandy induced headache.

He tapped his fingers against the banister of the mezzanine. A few women tilted their heads toward him, fluttering their lashes and elbowing their neighbors. Diamonds and rubies gleamed from their throats and their coiffured curls remained immaculate. Jasper shot them his customary wide smile. He didn't wait long for them to flap their fans. This game had seemed more interesting when he'd been new to London. Normally, he would go and make their acquaintances, or, in most cases now, remake them, but an odd ennui hampered his customary actions.

Still, he couldn't linger on the mezzanine the whole night. He descended the stairs and entered the crowd.

One of his footmen approached him. "I have a note for you, Your Grace."

Balls were not the customary place to receive correspondence, but Jasper extended his hand.

The footman's shoulders eased, and he hastened away.

Jasper read the note. He didn't recognize the handwriting and he strode toward the footman, rejoining him quickly. "I'm to go to my room?"

"I—er—suppose." The servant averted his gaze.

"Who gave you this?"

"Is it important?" The footman's voice trembled, and he shrank back with an odd air of guilt.

Jasper sighed. The footman was new, and even though Jasper strove not to intimidate his staff, his title made the process difficult.

"Don't worry," Jasper assured the man.

His curiosity was, after all, officially piqued. Had a widow arranged a tête-à-tête? More likely one of his friends wanted to laud the charms of one of the women here and strategize about how to win her heart.

Jasper strolled through the ballroom, moving through the crush of revelers. Men from his schooldays slapped him on the back, beaming jovially, as if they still couldn't believe they'd reached an age in which they might drink and dance with delight; a world in which arithmetic and geography lessons no longer existed and where no one would cane them for an incorrect Latin declension. Debutantes tittered when they viewed him, tossing their hair so their carefully curled ringlets caught the light.

Finally, he left the ballroom, and Jasper shivered.

Obviously, the temperature had fallen.

Obviously, he was not shivering because of some premonition, even if he did wonder why he'd been summoned to his bedroom.

He nodded to the butler, then ascended the staircase. The sound of the music grew faint, but as he entered the dark corridor, the ballroom door slammed below. Evidently, he wasn't the only person who'd abandoned the festivity, even if the hour remained early. Jasper trod over the familiar oriental carpets, past the familiar gilded-legged sideboards until he reached his room.

This is foolish.

He should have ignored the message. Still, he may as well investigate

Jasper pushed open the door and blinked into the dim light. A scent of roses drifted through the room. Behind him footsteps sounded, and soprano and baritone voices murmured.

On another occasion he might have chuckled, wondering if the two people were finding a spare room in which they might have a tryst. It wouldn't be the first time people had engaged in passion at one of his parties. Jasper excelled at creating a pleasant atmosphere that would inspire amorous pursuits.

"Help!" a woman called.

Jasper blinked.

This was hardly Shoreditch.

Nobody should require assistance in his home.

"Quickly," the woman added.

Jasper turned toward the voice.

The sound came from his bed.

"Help!" the voice repeated.

Jasper might be confused, but he could still act like a gentleman. He approached her with speed.

Normally if a woman called him to his bed, it was so he might touch her *there* and *there* and *at once*. Despite the woman's urgent tone, and its resemblance to past bedside escapades, Jasper doubted this woman desired that.

After all, he didn't recognize her voice.

He grabbed a candle and lit a match, casting light toward the bed.

There was indeed a woman on his bed. She lay in a half-clothed state. Dark locks spilled over her shoulders.

The sight was not entirely uncommon, even if he'd reduced such instances since his friend Hugh had married.

But this woman's hands were tied to his bedposts.

Strange.

He blinked.

The woman resembled Miss Margaret Carberry.

Very strange.

Of all the women he might find on his bed, he would not have expected Miss Carberry. He'd met her at a house party, and he remembered her as a rigid wallflower, one who found even the prospect of making conversation daunting, who had yet to master the not-so-very-difficult rules of small talk.

But then she'd been dressed primly. Unlike her companions she hadn't shown any eagerness to make conversation with him. She'd never fluttered her lashes. Indeed, if anything she'd seemed eager to drift into the background.

But Miss Carberry was certainly noticeable now.

A distinct smell of champagne wafted toward him, and long curly hair framed her face in an appealing manner. She was clothed in a yellow dress, though his attention was drawn to a deep tear in her gown that revealed delicious skin.

"Miss Carberry?"

"Please untie me," she ordered.

He forced himself to withdraw his gaze from her and banish the image of her rounded chest, no matter how alluring it was.

Why was she here? Miss Carberry had always seemed practical. If she were attempting to seduce him, she wouldn't be eager to leave the bed.

He scrunched his forehead. An atrocious thought entered his mind.

"Did someone harm you?" He shifted his legs, not wanting to contemplate that one of his guests might have acted so vilely. "Because if you tell me his name, I assure you I will do my utmost to—"

"No," she said hastily. "Nothing like that."

He blinked again.

"This is not the time for explanations," she said.

Jasper might like to chatter, but he knew when his conversation was undesired. He hurried toward the bed, removed a knife from his bedside drawer, and hastily freed her.

"Thank you." She leaped from the four-poster bed into a pile of rose petals. Her hair was messy, and thick curls cascaded from her chignon.

She didn't flutter her eyelashes at him. Instead, her eyes darted wildly.

"What is the meaning of this?" a strange man's voice demanded.

Miss Carberry ducked down, and her large bosom bounced. Jasper's throat dried, and he vowed to not muse on her plump globes.

"Oh, please come!" a female voice wailed. "Hurry! My daughter is here. Alone with the duke."

"Goodness gracious," the man said. "Are you certain?"

"Naturally!"

Jasper jerked his head to the side.

What were those people talking about? Miss Carberry crawled on the carpet as if she were a French spy. Rose petals stuck in her hair.

Blast it, there was no reason for rose petals to be on the floor.

Miss Carberry hadn't just been tied to the bed—her dress was torn.

As if I tore it while ravishing her.

Jasper's fist tightened.

Damnation.

It was happening: the thing all aristocrats feared. He was being framed to appear as if he'd compromised a woman.

Jasper had met Miss Carberry's mother. She'd thrust Miss Carberry toward his friend Hugh, the Marquess of Metcalfe. Now the marquess had married, perhaps Mrs. Carberry had decided to direct her attention to Jasper.

Double damnation.

"They can't find me here," Miss Carberry whispered and she sprinted toward the window.

"What are you doing?" Jasper asked.

A man wasn't supposed to find it normal to find chits tied to his bed. It was the sort of thing that would make any man—even the worldly, sophisticated sort—have questions.

Questions Miss Carberry seemed in no mood to answer.

"They're coming." Miss Carberry scurried behind the curtain.

The door opened, and Jasper turned his head.

Two people stormed in: a sterner, older looking version of the woman he'd just seen, whom he recognized as Mrs. Carberry, and another man, wearing a white collar.

Blast.

The chit's mother had dragged a man of the cloth with her: a *bishop.* The word of a man who adhered to morals and ethics, or one who at least advocated for others to adhere to morals and ethics, would be taken seriously. No one liked to contradict bishops, not if one didn't have a peculiar delight in perpetual flames, distracted only by the screams of unhappy residents and horn-adorned creatures brandishing pitchforks.

"She's here!" Mrs. Carberry flourished her hand in the direction of the four-poster bed. Her bracelets jangled, and her voice had an odd triumphant ring. The sound did not resemble the anguish he'd imagined someone might feel who believed their daughter actually *had* been compromised.

No, her voice was distinctly smug.

And now her daughter was subjected to huddling outside his window.

Jasper hadn't possessed much of an opinion of Mrs. Carberry when he'd met her before. He instantly revised his opinion and placed her in the negative column, settling her only above charging French soldiers.

"What are you speaking about?" Jasper asked in an icy tone he preferred not to employ, favoring a more warm-hearted approach to others. This, though, was the moment for aristocratic aloofness.

Mrs. Carberry widened her eyes, then her face paled.

"You are in my chambers," Jasper said. "And I did *not* invite you."

"Er—yes." Mrs. Carberry retained her gaze on the bed.

"This woman said a young lady was here against her will," the bishop said hesitantly.

"She was mistaken, my lord," Jasper said. "I am alone. Perhaps she succumbed to a daydream. Despite its name, one does not require it to be day to experience one."

"I did not imagine the calamity," Mrs. Carberry huffed.

The bishop looked dubiously at her. He furrowed his ample forehead, unburdened by any hair. "This is most odd. Most odd, indeed."

"A commendable observation," Jasper said. "Most astute. But then again, is not life filled with oddities?"

A frown descended upon the bishop's face. "Your Grace, I prefer to see the world as marvelous, filled with the manifestations of the Lord."

"Quite, quite," Jasper said quickly.

Entering a theological conversation while a perfectly good ball was going on downstairs, not to speak of the woman tucked on the other side of the drapes, did not top Jasper's immediate desires. Right now, the only thing he wanted was a generously poured drink.

"These mistakes happen," Jasper said graciously, even if this particular occurrence had never happened to him before, and it hardly seemed unintentional. He headed toward the door. "Now, let's go downstairs. I assure you the ball is more interesting."

The bishop followed him obediently, but Mrs. Carberry halted.

Jasper's heart sank.

A woman willing to tie her daughter to a duke's bed was unlikely to be daunted by the temporary absence of said daughter.

"But she was here!" Mrs. Carberry insisted. "Look. The bed is...rumpled!"

"I hope you're not insulting the work of my chamber maid?" Jasper asked.

"Nonsense," Mrs. Carberry said. "I am complimenting them. I doubt they would have left such an indention."

"That does sound like a compliment, Your Grace," the bishop said cheerfully.

"I think I sat on the bed," Jasper said.

"You think?" the bishop asked.

"I'm quite certain," Jasper amended. "Absolutely certain."

The bishop did not seem aware of the fact that 'absolutely' was a word that denoted confidence, for the bishop's forehead crinkled again. "You did not desire to attend your own ball?"

"I've just arrived," Jasper said. "Besides, why merry-make when one can contemplate the miraculousness of life?"

"Quite right," the bishop said. "You are a wise man, Your Grace."

"He is a man hiding my daughter," Mrs. Carberry exclaimed. "Margaret! Margaret! Where are you?"

For a moment, Jasper thought Miss Carberry might poke her head out from behind the curtain, but no sound drifted from the window.

"She's not here," Jasper said. "Obviously."

"We truly must leave," the bishop urged his companion. "Lingering in the duke's private chambers is inappropriate."

Mrs. Carberry sniffed. "I refuse to take societal etiquette lessons from a bishop. He must have hidden her somewhere."

"I do not hide women in my bedroom," Jasper said stiffly.

"Perhaps she's in your wardrobe," Mrs. Carberry said.

"An abominable suggestion," the bishop said. "Please, do not embarrass yourself. We would not want the duke to think poorly of you."

Mrs. Carberry hesitated, doubtlessly contemplating the consequences of lingering, but finally, she shook her head firmly.

Jasper's heart sank.

Perhaps Mrs. Carberry thought she'd already hindered her place on the list of invitees for future festivities. If she found her daughter, that would ensure an elevated status.

"Nevertheless, I shall look." Mrs. Carberry strode toward the wardrobe, swung it open, stared at the rows of tailcoats and trousers, and quickly slammed it shut. "Not here."

"Precisely," Jasper said. "I would not harm your daughter."

Mrs. Carberry sniffed and ducked her head below the bed. Her face had reddened, bearing a resemblance to a strawberry, but she continued to search the room.

Jasper almost admired her resolve.

"Perhaps she's behind the curtains!" Mrs. Carberry marched toward the window.

"N-No," Jasper said.

If Mrs. Carberry found her, as she certainly would, the bishop would become suspicious. No doubt he'd announce an immediate need for Jasper to post the banns. With Jasper's current luck, the bishop might be seeing the Archbishop of Canterbury the next day and would begin the arrangements for a special license.

"That's not necessary," Jasper blurted.

"On the contrary, it's *quite* necessary," Mrs. Carberry replied.

Though Jasper's bedroom was of a generous proportion, and though Mrs. Carberry's legs were of the short variety, it did not take Mrs. Carberry long to reach the window.

"I'd rather you wouldn't look," Jasper said.

Mrs. Carberry's lips formed a straight line, and she drew the curtain.

No woman was behind it.

Jasper's mouth dropped open. Miss Carberry should be standing right outside. No stairs descended from the balcony.

Where the bloody hell had she gone?

CHAPTER THREE

WIND SLAMMED AGAINST Margaret. Even though the wind had seemed unremarkable when Margaret had queued outside, ranking lower in irritation than the incessant drizzle, now it was impossible to ignore. If only the duke had decided to shatter tradition and have a ground floor bedroom. Margaret had known she shouldn't exit the window, even before she'd seen the exact manner in which the duke's majestic eyebrows had lurched toward his artfully tousled hair.

One didn't clamber from bedroom windows.

But then, one also shouldn't be tied to bedposts.

Somehow, her actions had seemed appropriate, but an appreciation for the practicableness of stairs and the reasons for their decided popularity swept through her. Facade clambering was not a common occupation, even for the athletic.

Margaret was not athletic. Running only irritated her generously sized bosom, and doing other exercises, which involved bending and contorting her body into odd positions, made her feel ridiculous.

And yet, here she was, on a narrow balcony.

She glanced down. Guests no longer queued outside the townhouse. The last thing Margaret needed was for someone to spot her and yell "thief." Even worse would be if someone *recognized* her. There was no explanation possible for why a debutante might be on the balcony that led to a duke's bedroom. After all, no chaperone, was beside her. Not even Grandmother Agatha, whom she normally managed to wrangle to accompany her on visits that were of less interest to her mother.

Margaret assessed the situation. The problem with clinging onto a balcony was the now chilly air. The wind slammed against her, pulling her canary-colored dress, as if delighted to have so much fabric with which to play. Even if it had chosen to be less active, the frigid air would still be galling.

Below her, carriages continued to drive past, sometimes dropping off passengers, or sometimes picking up the ones who contented themselves with making a brief appearance before a long night of drifting from party to party.

Rain dabbled down, sliding over her fingers. She'd already destroyed her lace gloves trying to break her restraints.

Margaret was glad she couldn't see the duke's expression—but even if she couldn't see his face, she knew he must be aghast.

Margaret shifted her legs. Voices sounded from below, and she scrunched against the balcony, wishing the architect had designed the facade with less enthusiasm for columns. One hardly needed a building to resemble a Greek temple when—even in Greece—people had stopped worshiping their gods centuries ago.

Her mother's voice rang out. She was going to search on the balcony.

Margaret's heart spun, careening this way and that, uncaring about her other body vessels. Breathing grew difficult.

She needed to hide.

At once.

Unfortunately, balconies made atrocious hiding spots.

An idea shot through her.

Margaret hastily climbed over the balcony rail and placed her feet on the brick header to her left.

It worked, and Margaret beamed. Other women might have been afraid of the lack of stability, but Margaret had done it. She clung onto the iron rails of the balcony, and now if her mother opened the door—*when* her mother opened the door—she would be hidden.

It was perfect.

The rain continued to splatter onto her face and hands; it continued to dampen her dress, but it didn't matter. Half an hour ago, she'd been certain she would have to marry the duke. And though the man had shown no signs of cruelty, she had no desire to marry a man forced to become her husband. He would always know he was a duke, and that she was a wallflower dragooned into society by the sheer force of her father's sudden supply of coin.

"Oy! Up there!" a man shouted.

Margaret froze. Her dress was unlikely to blend into the brick walls, and she cursed the fact that the Duke of Jevington had not possessed an eccentric manner that had compelled him to order the bricks to be painted to match the sun. Instead, the house resembled the other townhouses on the block. Only the exact composition of columns and flourishes differed.

"Get down, girl. It's dangerous up there!" the man yelled.

Oh, dear.

The wind blustered but failed to swallow the man's voice. Any moment now her mother might investigate.

That moment would arrive sooner if the man continued to flaunt his diaphragm capabilities.

Margaret flung her gaze downward. It was easy to spot him. He wore a cloak and top hat, familiar livery for a driver.

She twisted her torso inelegantly toward the man, even though turning when one's feet needed to remain on a brick header above a window and one's hands needed to be clutching onto balcony rails must be one of the great foolish things to do. If only she'd taken a greater interest in athletic conditioning. She'd always scoffed at the women who deemed such maneuvers the pinnacle of their day, favoring the joys of memorizing new facts.

She placed her finger over her lips, hoping he'd be quiet.

"Careful, lady!" the man hollered.

She repeated the gesture.

"Did you see that woman?" the man yelled, turning his head.

Margaret cringed.

The man wasn't the sole person outside. No doubt in a few minutes he'd have every driver staring at her. Worse, he might have the butler out there staring at her.

"Quiet!" she mouthed.

The balcony door opened, and she froze. Then it slammed shut, before the man could shout again, and relief thrummed through her.

She was safe.

She attempted to adjust her position, so she could clamber up to the balcony and wait until her mother left the duke's room. A gust of wind nearly toppled her, seeming desirous of forcing the tear in her dress to increase in indecency.

Her fingers slipped. She struggled to retighten her grip, but more rain landed, swathing her hand in icy liquid.

Her heart leaped uncertainly, but she gritted her teeth.

I can do this.

I have *to do this.*

Margaret concentrated on tightening her grip around the rail, not caring how ridiculous she might appear from the street.

She couldn't let go.

Letting go might mean injury.

Letting go might mean *death.*

"Hang on, dearie!" the man shouted. "Don't fall. You don't want to kill yourself."

The man's hollers lacked reassurance.

"That girl's about to die," he said loudly. "Right on Grosvenor Square. Imagine that. Not worth it being a thief, no it ain't."

Margaret's heart lurched in her chest, and the cold rain continued to pelt her. Raindrops slid under her neckline, trickling over her back with more force than the champagne had succeeded in doing.

Her teeth chattered, but she held on.

More voices sounded under her, carriage wheels rumbled, and a horse neighed, but she held on.

The process remained difficult. Exhaustion ratcheted through her, and pain shot through her arm. Wind blustered against her, whipping ringlets of hair over her eyes.

Her fingers slipped.

Fiddle-faddle.

Margaret plummeted.

She flung her hands into the air, attempting to clasp onto something, anything.

Her locks swept away from her eyes, but all she saw was grayness.

She flailed her arms upward, as if there might possibly be anything to grasp, but there was nothing: this was the end.

Margaret crashed.

She bounced.

Bouncing was not the outcome she'd expected. She rolled, then fell more, this time landing on cobblestones.

She was alive. It was a state she'd taken for granted, but which she now very much appreciated.

Cold raindrops continued to land on her, her body ached, and her dress was now both torn and muddied, but it didn't matter.

I'm alive.

She sighed.

Blissfully.

"Miss?" The stern-looking butler from earlier dashed from a carriage, followed by the talkative driver, who was on the pavement.

She scrambled from the cobblestones. Her feathered turban had landed in a muddy puddle, and a feather had snapped from its perch. Though she'd desired an excuse not to wear it, the vision of the destroyed turban lacked the satisfaction she'd envisioned.

The butler scrutinized her with the vigor of a man accustomed to searching for the slightest smudges when polishing silver. "Are you well?"

"Yes." She was fine. She was standing, and her hands worked.

Margaret surveyed the carriage. Evidently, she'd landed on the carriage's roof and that had saved her. "You moved that for me?"

The butler nodded. "After that man alerted me, I contemplated going indoors and reaching you from the balcony, but I thought this would be quicker."

"Thank you," she said.

"You could have ruined that carriage," the driver barked. "Glad it ain't mine." He cast a stern glance at the butler. "Carriages are expensive."

"I-I didn't mean to fall," Margaret stammered.

The driver furrowed thick brows and glared.

He turned to the butler. "Shall I look for a night watchman? Perhaps she was trying to steal! Awfully nice dress for a vagrant. Most suspicious."

The butler gave a gentle smile. "I believe she is a guest, sir."

"A guest?" The driver's eyes rounded. "Are you certain?"

"It is hard to forget a dress of that particular shade of yellow. The same goes for that turban." The butler moved his gaze solemnly toward the puddle and its ruined contents.

The men continued to speak, but Margaret couldn't listen. She needed to leave.

Even the most eccentric weren't supposed to clamber outside ducal balconies. Margaret hadn't survived so she could be berated more. Her status in society already sufficed in lowness. She hardly required rumors she was a thief. She couldn't stay here, but she couldn't enter the ball with a muddied, torn dress either.

Drivers gazed at her curiously from their carriages, some moving their heads into the drizzle of rain.

If only her driver were lingering here. Unfortunately, he was going to pick them up at midnight. The sky might be dark, but she doubted it was anywhere near that time yet, and Margaret had no desire to wait for him.

"Would you like to go inside?" the butler asked.

Margaret hesitated.

Not remaining in the rain was tempting. She shouldn't remain here and continue to have conversations with bemused drivers. At any moment a guest might exit the townhouse. Margaret's presence would be impossible to not notice, and Margaret's reputation would become even more questionable.

Perhaps Margaret had not been discovered bedding the duke, but standing on a street in a torn, tattered dress alone was not a great improvement.

And yet...

Even if she could absolutely not linger outside, unfortunately, she could not venture inside. Without question she would encounter *more* members of the *ton* inside.

She squeezed her eyes.

Her mother had succeeded in ruining her after all, and all Margaret had accomplished was to make certain the Duke of Jevington was not involved in any scandal.

She frowned.

She was in Grosvenor Square.

Daisy lived nearby.

Margaret could visit her, since Daisy wouldn't be at the ball.

"You really should step inside," the butler said gently.

"I should be hauling her off to determine she ain't no criminal," the driver said. "Not good when a woman can burgle a house in a nice neighborhood like this."

"I wasn't going to steal," Margaret protested.

"Then just what were you trying to do?" the driver asked. "Seems to me you must have been trying to do that, even if you did have an invitation."

Margaret stared at him.

The butler and driver stared at her.

Right.

Margaret shifted her legs.

"Must be a professional too," the driver mused, "given as how I didn't even notice her climb up."

There was no time for further musings, no matter how valuable the process of thinking normally was. Instead, Margaret bolted.

She lifted her skirt to avoid stepping on the hem and scurried down the street. She avoided looking at the carriages, as if not catching the drivers' eyes might mean they would not spot a flurry of canary yellow and brunette locks.

She fled past Grosvenor Square, then turned onto one side street, then another. Too late, she realized she didn't even have a reticule and had no money for a hack.

She gritted her teeth.

She wasn't looking for a hack—yet.

She was looking for Daisy.

Finally, she arrived at her friend's townhouse.

She considered clambering through her friend's window. But unlike in Loretta Van Lochen novels, she didn't trust herself to scale the building. Even the duke's balcony had proved perilous.

Besides, Daisy was sensible and unlikely to have her window open. This part of Mayfair might be pleasant, but this remained London, and many people in need of coin were aware of its abundance in this neighborhood.

Margaret smoothed her dress, conscious mud remained caked on various parts. Dress smoothing hardly compared with dress washing, drying and pressing, but it would have to suffice.

She grabbed the knocker, tapped it, and eventually, the butler opened the door.

If he was indignant at having been interrupted from his plans to sleep, he did not verbalize them. He did though widen his eyes and curl his lips.

"I'm so sorry," she rushed to say. "But I wanted to speak with Miss Holloway."

The butler frowned, and she shivered under his steely gaze.

"Is she in?" Margaret's voice trembled.

"Miss Holloway is not prone to cavorting about the city at odd hours of the night." The butler's voice boomed in an authoritative tone. No doubt he was successful at keeping the footmen in check, perhaps even appearing in their dreams after particularly clumsy serving incidents.

Margaret shuddered, as if he were a ship's captain who'd just announced that the ship's mast had toppled into the ocean and survival was uncertain.

"But may I see her?"

The butler exhaled, and his confident manner appeared flummoxed. "These are not regular calling hours, young lady."

Thumping sounded upstairs, and Margaret suddenly was grateful for the strength of the butler's voice, after all.

"Oh, Jameson," Daisy called from the mezzanine. "You needn't pretend to be a guard dog. It's only Miss Carberry."

"You haven't seen her attire," Jameson murmured, and his lips twisted in that particular manner common to people who had discovered the perfect retort, and were contriving, for continued employment purposes, not to utter their witticisms.

Daisy waved her hand through the bannister. "Don't mind him. Come on up."

Margaret nodded and hurried up the stairs. Daisy's mouth fell when Margaret approached. Evidently, she'd noticed her attire.

"I suppose you would like to chat."

"Er—yes."

Daisy turned her chair and wheeled toward her bedroom. Margaret followed hastily after her.

"It is nice for you to pay me a call," Daisy said.

A grandfather clock ticked forcefully.

"I'm sorry about the late time," Margaret said.

"Nonsense," Daisy said cheerfully. "I was simply reading. Though I do adore *Sense and Sensibility,* I no longer worry Edmund will forget Elinor entirely, and the task no longer takes on the same urgency."

A door opened, and Mrs. Holloway stuck out her head. Her blonde curls were covered with a cap, and her matching blonde eyebrows leaped upward. "Miss Carberry?"

Margaret's throat dried, but she managed to dip into a hasty curtsy. "Pleased to see you."

"Of course." Mrs. Holloway's gaze drifted to Margaret's dress. "This is quite late."

"I know," Margaret said apologetically. "I'm afraid it's urgent."

Arriving at a friend's house at a late hour was a definite etiquette breach, even if the thickest tomes devoted to the subject might fail to explicitly warn against it. Their pages were devoted to sternly worded cautions on the irreparable harm that might ensue after succumbing to a grievous mishap by picking up the wrong fork.

No, Margaret was certain she had made a deep breach of civility.

Mrs. Holloway scrutinized her cautiously. "Does your mother know you're here?"

Mama. Margaret's fingers fluttered. What was her mother doing now? Was she continuing to search? Margaret hoped she had the sense not to. The last thing she needed was for her mother to inform everyone at a ball that Margaret was ruined, when she had no proof and thus, there could never be a marriage.

No. Her mother was in possession of *some* sense. Perhaps her mother was worrying, but truly, Margaret refused to feel guilty. Not after what had happened.

"I'll take that lengthy pause as a no," Mrs. Holloway said.

Margaret's cheeks warmed. "I assure you I really do have quite an urgent matter to discuss."

Mrs. Holloway shifted her legs. Her discomfort was palpable, as if she'd reached the most complex moment in her childrearing journey. "Don't get involved, Daisy."

"Mama!" Daisy groaned. "Margaret hardly goes around participating in illicit activities."

"I suppose that would be uncharacteristic," Mrs. Holloway said finally, her gaze fixed on Margaret's dress, as if considering the fact that Margaret's untamed appearance was also uncharacteristic.

Though Margaret's appearance never achieved glossy perfection— her thick locks slipped from her pins no matter how much time was spent arranging them, and her dress managed to become consistently creased—she normally looked more respectable.

Finally, Mrs. Holloway sighed. "Just be quick."

Daisy beamed. "Of course."

CHAPTER FOUR

"YOU'VE GOT DREADFULLY good luck." Daisy declared, wheeling her chair toward her bedroom. "Papa's at his club."

The walls inside Daisy's bedroom were painted a cheerful tangerine, and Margaret exhaled. If her dress weren't destroyed, this would almost seem normal.

Daisy's mother wouldn't let Margaret stay for long. Margaret couldn't have the luxury of postponing this conversation, no matter how unpleasant recollecting the experience was, and no matter how little she desired to see pity in her friend's gaze.

Margaret was frequently pitied. More pity was intolerable.

Daisy swung the door shut, and her bright blue eyes gleamed. "Reveal everything. Disclose your secrets. Lay out your skeletons."

"No skeletons," Margaret blurted.

"Pity. My parents won't let me have a real one, and I wouldn't mind a metaphorical one."

Daisy's interest in medicine was renowned, but Margaret still shuddered. Skeletons could remain in neatly groomed cemeteries, underneath equally neatly shaped tombstones and, on special occasions, adorned with tasteful selections of flowers.

Daisy rotated her wheelchair against the wall. "You came from the ball. Was it as dreadful as you imagined?"

Margaret settled into a chair. "Worse."

Daisy shivered. "The nice thing about being friends with you is that I do not feel I'm missing out. Now what happened? Were you confined to the smoky wallflower section beside the chimney?"

"Worse."

Daisy's eyes widened. "You weren't dancing the whole time, were you? Making a spectacle of yourself with your inelegant dance steps."

Margaret drew herself up. "How do you know my dance steps are imperfect?"

Daisy smirked. "I've seen you walk."

Margaret scowled. But it was true: she was a dreadful dancer, no matter how much her instructors corrected her, no matter how effusively they beseeched her to improve, and no matter how much Margaret desired to do just that.

"I wasn't dancing," Margaret said sullenly, crossing her arms.

"But you did attend the ball?" Daisy gazed at Margaret's dress, as if pondering whether she may have fallen into a muddy puddle and only just managed to drag herself out.

"Naturally." Margaret raised her chin. "Besides, Mama would never have stood for not attending."

Daisy was silent, her gaze intelligent. This was the moment to disclose everything, but Margaret found her heart clenching as if desiring to stomp out her vocal cords.

Finally, Margaret sighed. "I wasn't by the fire, and I wasn't dancing. I—er—was on the duke's bed."

Daisy's mouth dropped open.

"So I wasn't uncomfortable," Margaret continued with an odd laugh. "The bed was soft."

"And you were truly in *his* bed? Not a guest room?"

"Oh, the duke was present too."

Daisy remained silent, though her eyebrows leaped upward.

"I mean, he wasn't present the whole time," Margaret explained. "That would be inappropriate."

"I suppose there's a limit to inappropriateness," Daisy said faintly.

"Precisely," Margaret agreed. "I didn't choose to be on his bed."

"Did he sweep you up and put you there? Is the duke's by-blow going to make an appearance in nine months?"

"Nonsense. He didn't touch me."

Daisy looked at her strangely. "Did your mother by any chance place you on the bed?"

Margaret gave a miserable nod, and Daisy's eyes welled.

Margaret averted her gaze. "She had help."

"But she orchestrated it?"

"Yes." Margaret's voice squeaked. "She brought a bishop to 'discover' us."

"She meant for the Duke of Jevington to be accused of compromising you?"

"Indeed."

"And her plan didn't work," Daisy said gently.

"Precisely."

Daisy squeezed her hand sympathetically, but then giggled. "So, the duke found you on his bed?"

"It's not amusing," Margaret said.

"Are you certain?" Daisy's eyes gleamed, and Margaret felt her lips twitching.

"How did he react? Did he touch you?"

"He touched my wrists, but that was because I asked him too."

"If I were alone with him, I would ask him to touch more than my wrists," Daisy breathed.

Margaret widened her eyes, and Daisy's cheeks pinkened.

"It wasn't a matter of pleasure," Margaret said hastily. "Naturally!"

"Naturally," Daisy repeated with an air of dubiousness.

"I was restrained to his bed. Obviously, when he entered, I had to ask him to untie me. And the best location to put restraints has always been on one's wrists. Something about making it hard to use one's hands."

"Hands are quite important," Daisy agreed.

"Yes. I suppose it would be far more uncomfortable if they went about tying people's chests."

"Ah, the bovine technique."

Margaret shot her friend a quizzical glance.

"Normally rendered by cowboys with the use of something called a lasso," Daisy added.

For the moment they were silent, contemplating the eccentricities prevalent in Britain's former colonies. On another night, Margaret might have added a comment about the passionate American distaste for tea, but this was no time for small talk, even of the indubitably interesting sort.

"I climbed out the window and ran away," Margaret said. "She's probably upset."

"She's probably outraged. Most women would have stayed there. You could have nabbed a duke."

Margaret sighed. "Nobody would have believed he was compromising me, anyway."

"I don't believe that's true."

"O-Of course it is," Margaret stammered.

Perhaps Daisy didn't see how other people interacted with Margaret, but Margaret did. She was a wallflower, and wallflowers never bedded dukes.

"The duke would have declared that my mother and I staged a false compromising situation," Margaret said. "And everyone would have believed him"

It was obvious.

Utterly.

Daisy tilted her head, shifting her long blond strands. Perhaps she'd interrupted Daisy brushing her hair.

It was late, and Margaret shouldn't be here. If only her parents had bought a house in Mayfair, instead of their large townhouse with its unusually large garden. If only Margaret could have gone straight home.

"Perhaps he wouldn't have done that," Daisy said.

"I couldn't force him to marry me. I couldn't begin married life that way."

"Of course not," Daisy said, her voice warm. "And that's the real reason you're my dearest friend. And the reason the duke would have been lucky to have been forced to marry you."

"Nonsense," Margaret said.

The duke could marry anyone. He shouldn't be saddled with a woman everyone was happy to dismiss.

She shook her head. "I'm sorry. I had no intention of coming here and being despondent. I'm—er—afraid I lost my reticule. Not that I had much coin in it any way. Do you think I might borrow fare for a hack?"

Daisy straightened. "You intend to return home?"

Margaret nodded.

"After what your mother did?" A strange outrage sounded in Daisy's voice, an expression that Margaret did not associate with Daisy's normally pleasant disposition.

Margaret nodded again. "Of course."

"I'm certain my mother will put you up."

Margaret raised her eyebrows.

"Well." Daisy looked down as her cheeks pinkened, before she raised her gaze and leaned toward Margaret. "We don't *have* to tell her."

Margaret giggled. "I'm sure she's eagerly waiting for me to leave."

"You can climb up the window," Daisy said.

"Last time I fell."

"You can't fall *every* time."

"I doubt dark will improve my abilities."

"Then we shall tell her," Daisy amended. "Obviously, you can't go back. Who knows what your mother will do next?"

Margaret frowned momentarily. Then she raised her chin in that time-honored tradition of people intent on making the best of dubious circumstances. The gesture might have dubious wish fulfilling merits, but nevertheless, Margaret vowed to not worry. "All I need is a plan. Well, all I need is a *good* plan. And then I can move from my home and live happily ever after."

Margaret was not going to let her mother continue to take control of her life. Not when her mother's plan involved tying her to beds.

"What you need," Daisy said, "is to marry."

Margaret gazed at her friend suspiciously.

Normally, Daisy displayed a reasonableness that Margaret appreciated. Margaret had never thought Daisy was given to uttering maddening statements, and it was unfortunate that Daisy had apparently lost her sense at this precise moment.

"I'm not going to claim that the duke compromised me."

"Then don't marry the duke," Daisy said. "But remember, if you marry, you won't be subjected to your mother's crazed attempts."

Margaret frowned. Technically, Daisy might have a point. Her mother *had* bribed someone before the season began to laud her to the Marquess of Metcalfe. Unfortunately for Margaret's mother, the woman she'd chosen had ended up marrying the marquess. Mama had dragged Margaret to every ball this season, sometimes shuttling her to a different one before Margaret had even had a chance to test the canapes. All Mama's work hadn't mattered: no one was courting Margaret. Perhaps no one ever would.

"No one will marry me," Margaret said. "That's why I'm in this situation."

"Your 'being tied to bedposts' situation?" Daisy's lips twitched.

Margaret crossed her arms. "It's not amusing."

Daisy raised an eyebrow, and Margaret sighed.

Perhaps it was amusing.

Even if the incident had been terribly awkward.

"I don't want to marry just anyone," Margaret said. "I have standards."

"And so you should," Daisy said.

Margaret scrutinized her friend. For some reason, Daisy continued to smile and nod, as if they were having a normal conversation; as if her friend was entirely incognizant that every word she uttered was of the nonsensical variety.

"No one wants to marry a Scottish woman whose father is in trade. When people make conversation, they wonder that I've been invited at all."

"It's because your father is very rich."

"I know, but—"

Daisy shook her head. "You'll be fine."

Margaret considered telling her that every word was absurd. Naturally, Margaret wouldn't be fine. Men were not known to rave about the frizziness of overly thick hair or the lack of a willowy figure.

"Men don't want to court me."

"Precisely." Daisy beamed. "Which is why you'll need to rapidly advance your social position."

Margaret narrowed her eyes. Daisy blithely discussed the impossible. If Margaret had been able to rapidly advance her social position, Papa's money would have seen to that.

"You just need some help," Daisy mused.

"Mothers are supposed to help," Margaret said.

"Well, yes. But yours is rather too enthusiastic in the fulfillment of her duties. But perhaps..." Daisy was silent, then a smile frolicked over her lips.

Margaret stiffened as Daisy's smile continued to grow, harboring all manner of ominousness. Only truly absurd thoughts might cause Daisy's lips to extend to such a high manner or for her eyes to gleam with such foreboding.

Daisy leaned forward. "There is someone else who can help."

"I hope you're not going to volunteer your mother."

"Nonsense. She wouldn't be sufficiently motivated."

"But who would be?"

"The Duke of Jevington."

Margaret blinked.

She opened her mouth to speak, but words failed her. They seemed to have been extinguished by the mere absurdity of Daisy's statement. Finally, she shook her head.

"It's true." Daisy leaned back confidently.

"You haven't met him. He wouldn't help me."

"He was probably exceedingly grateful you didn't stay in his room. You could be making preparations for becoming a duchess. Instead, you're here. Not quite as lofty a location." She smiled wryly.

Daisy's home might be in a pleasant neighborhood, but the interior lacked the lavishness of some of Margaret's other friends. No Roman busts perched on sideboards, and no Grecian goddesses stared down from elaborate painted ceilings. Daisy's home seemed...cozy. After all, her parents had devoted time to hauling her from spa to spa in the hopes of healing her lameness. None of the efforts had worked, despite her father's coffers and his eagerness to disperse coin. His coffers were rather less vast now, regrettably matching a similarly less buoyant spirit, and her mother hadn't confronted the task of wheedling for generous curtain budgets and lauding the merits of updated furniture with the same vigor as other women of the *ton*.

"I can't ask him to help me find a husband." Margaret scoffed at the notion.

"The Duke of Jevington isn't known to have a cruel reputation."

"He's also not known to have an insensible one."

Daisy didn't stiffen. Instead she removed her reticule from her desk, opened it up, and slipped some coin into Margaret's hand. "My parents insist I keep it for emergencies. Jameson will help you get a hack. And tomorrow, you will call on the duke and tell him of your predicament."

Despite the smooth drive of the carriage, now that London was dark and freed from its preponderance of hacks, wheelbarrows and people, Margaret returned home warily as she pondered her friend's words.

Finally, the carriage stopped before her family's townhouse. Margaret gazed at the forbidding building that loomed higher than the surrounding buildings, as if size could indicate grandeur. Her family had only moved there recently, and it felt as foreign as everything else in the capital.

Perhaps she should simply tell the driver to turn around and spend the night at Daisy's.

But that was hardly a permanent solution.

Not for the first time, Margaret wished she were home—her true home. Everything had been easier before Papa's business had taken off.

The driver opened the door, and Margaret exited the carriage. Her heart quivered, even though walking to the door was an action she'd done many times before, even though, normally, she was accompanied by either her mother or a maid.

Still, there was no point to tarry.

She raised her hand to the door knocker and tapped on it, wondering if the butler might have abandoned his post, given the late hour.

She need not have worried.

The door swung open immediately. Instead of the butler's solemn expression, her mother appeared.

"My dear child!" Mama shrieked, enveloping her in an embrace.

Mama normally did not hug her. Hugs were reserved for small children, not for daughters one feared might achieve spinsterhood.

"I was so worried," Mama squealed.

Margaret wondered whether she should remind her that she would not have been worried had she not decided to tie Margaret to the duke's bed.

Lily pattered toward her, wagging her tail, oblivious that this night was unlike any of the others. Margaret crouched down and petted her dog's pale coat.

"Ah, there you are," Papa said. Even though light gleamed from his *pince-nez* in their customary fashion, Margaret saw the friendly creases around his eyes, even if he displayed less emotion than her mother.

"Young lady, you should have come home with your mother," Papa said, as if remembering that this was a moment for parental showcasing, even if such moments were rare. "Why ever did you become separated from her?"

Mama looked at her nervously.

Margaret hesitated. Now was the time to tell her father everything, and yet, what would it accomplish? Papa might scold Mama?

No.

This was between her mother and herself. She just needed to be more careful, lest her mother decide to stage a false compromising scene again.

"I'm here now."

Papa nodded. "Right, right. So you are."

Another father might have become angry, with the air of a man who'd always pondered what it might be like to be a dictator and who took any misbehavior as a sign to fully explore that potential. Papa was not most men. When he halted his incessant meetings and perusals of various ledgers and reports, it was only to smile contentedly, as if he had a constant cup of chocolate in his hand. Papa was grateful for his good fortune and withstood the temptation lesser men had succumbed to of acting patronizing to everyone who'd not succeeded in becoming a titan.

Margaret shifted her legs. "I'll go upstairs."

"Quite sensible," Papa said. "I—er—should get back to my books."

Mama nodded, but there was an icy glint in her eyes, and when Margaret ascended the stairs, she wondered if she'd made a mistake in not saying everything.

CHAPTER FIVE

THE LIGHT MIGHT GLISTEN through his library, rendering the gold emblazoned letters on the vibrantly colored tomes even more magnificent than was their tendency, but Jasper's mind did not muse over the aesthetic pleasures of that event, nor did he contemplate with great delight the flavors of his bergamot and lemon tea. A peculiar feeling had lingered over him since escaping marriage, that most vile of institutions.

Jasper's closest proximity to leg-shackling before had been confined to some rather misty moments when reading Byron. Thankfully, no women had been present, and the mood had passed.

But he'd veered altogether too near to the dreaded marital institution. His heart beat oddly as he envisioned a life of quiet Sundays and pitter-pattering feet.

Actually, strictly speaking, quiet Sundays seemed an improvement to his current Sunday ritual of visiting the club. Hades' Lair was being converted into apartments, and Jasper now had to endure an unpleasant coach ride to enter a mediocre gaming hell. The armchairs might match a sumptuousness he'd thought only achieved by the leather armchairs at the now defunct Hades' Lair, but his friends had disappeared.

They'd married, one by one, vanishing as if some blasted maniacal killer had hacked each man apart.

Apparently, no such fate had occurred, even if Jasper eyed the crime section of the broadsheets with suspicion.

Jasper had attended their various weddings, at least the ones who'd not eloped in a shocking lack of judgement that should have gained instant admission to Bedlam. By all indications, his friends were now ensconced in the countryside, so as to gaze blissfully at fluffy lambs and plump flowers with greater ease. Hugh had even mused about the possibility of joining his wife in the art of watercolors.

Jasper scowled.

Other men might succumb to the sentimental drivel perpetuated by poets and depicted in oil smeared monstrosities by artists wielding blister inducing palettes. Jasper refused to succumb to other men's fates.

But I almost did.

Jasper focused on his correspondence. Picking up an envelope was normal, as was picking up an erasing knife to break the seal.

He scanned the contents, then frowned and rang the bell pull.

Powell soon appeared.

Jasper held up the letter in his hand. "This is a bill, Powell."

"Ah," Powell murmured. "Very good, Your Grace."

Jasper scrutinized his butler. "This is a bill to repair a carriage roof."

"I see, Your Grace." His butler shifted his legs.

"The Viscount of Brimfield indicates *you* ruined it." Jasper set the letter down. "Obviously, he must be mistaken."

Two pink circles appeared on his butler's cheeks. "I am afraid, Your Grace, that His Lordship is entirely correct."

Jasper drew his eyebrows together.

"You may subtract the fee from my wages," Powell said stoically with the sort of resigned expression painters were always employing when depicting men about to be executed.

"Was there a reason for you to destroy his carriage roof? Is it a new hobby of which I should be aware? Did the viscount say something particularly vile?" Jasper leaned forward and grinned. The viscount had a stodgy nature, and it was difficult to imagine him inspiring his always calm butler to take revenge. He was certain he'd never even heard the viscount curse.

"The viscount acted with his normal good grace," Powell said. "There was an incident with a young lady."

Jasper's eyebrows lurched up. He hadn't expected Powell to speak about a woman. Powell had seemed elderly when Jasper was a child and Powell was comforting him about his parents' and siblings' deaths. Powell hardly seemed susceptible to sneaking into carriages with women and engaging in vigorous activity that would lead to roof mutilation.

"The young lady in question was in danger of falling from a balcony. I surmised that she would find the landing less lethal were she to land on the viscount's carriage. The roof's surface is more conducive to comfort."

Jasper stared at his butler. "You saved her life."

Powell shrugged. "It was a pleasure."

"And that means—she almost lost hers." Jasper's heart lurched.

Powell gave him a sympathetic look.

"Blast it, she shouldn't have been in that position," Jasper exclaimed.

"Perhaps it will help you to know that she suffered no injuries."

"That's good." Jasper raked his hand through his hair. "I need to see her. I need to thank her."

Jasper searched for his address book.

"She had an invitation to the ball. I remember when she entered."

"Good, good." Jasper found the list.

"Will that be all, Your Grace?"

"For now," Jasper said, waving his hand up.

The butler nodded and left the room.

Jasper hastily found Miss Carberry's address.

Most women wouldn't hang off balconies, even if they were in the habit of reading adventurous gothics. They certainly weren't prone to risking their necks. Not when not risking their necks might mean an everlasting union with him.

It had been damned decent of her to risk her life. Damned foolish too.

Though Jasper had an appropriate disregard for his charms, he was aware that women had a habit of having glazed eyes in his presence, as if occupied with imagining unborn children.

Unborn children were always the perfect sort. They didn't glare grumpily at one, and they never tested their vocal range.

Debutantes were particularly prone to the malaise of misty eyes. When one had just been presented to the king, one was apt to imagine all sorts of things, even if nothing could be more ridiculous than picturing Jasper as a husband.

Evidently, Miss Carberry had seen the impossibility of any match quickly. Though Jasper was unsure whether he'd ever spoken to her, he *had* spent a house party with her. To be fair, Miss Carberry belonged to the shyer sort of woman, and she hadn't spoken much to anyone.

Miss Carberry's eagerness to avoid a marriage with him was almost insulting.

In fact, it was quite definitely insulting.

Had she thought he wouldn't do the right thing? Jasper might not be a marriage advocate, but he did not skirt his duties, even the one involving a morning church visit, an uncomfortable cravat knot and standing perilously near the altar while making eternal vows.

A knock sounded on the door, and his butler appeared. "You have a visitor, Your Grace."

"Thank you, Powell."

"I took the liberty of placing the young lady in the drawing room."

"Right. I'll just finish this letter—"

Powell coughed. "I believe you will want to see this lady."

Jasper swallowed hard. "Does the young lady have a name?"

"I am certain, Your Grace." Powell bowed. "Regrettably, I am not aware of it. She is not one of your normal visitors. She is, though, the lady who fell from the balcony last night."

Jasper's heart jolted, but he managed to retain a placid expression. "Very good, Powell."

"I should perhaps inform you that she brought another woman," the butler said.

"An older woman?" Jasper's voice trembled.

"That is an apt description of her, Your Grace."

Jasper jumped up, strode through the corridor and headed for the drawing room. His London townhouse might lack the bedroom count of his various castles, but it could hardly be described as compact. Finally, he entered the room.

On the chaise was Miss Margaret Carberry. Today, her dress had no tears, and was a somber navy blue compared to the garish yellow she'd favored yesterday, but it was definitely her. Beside her was an older woman with the gray hair and wrinkled skin his butler had mentioned.

Not Mrs. Carberry. Relief moved through him, and he returned his gaze to Miss Carberry.

"It's you," he said hoarsely.

"Er—yes." Her lips spread into an awkward smile that managed to be endearing.

Jasper bowed to the elderly looking woman beside her.

He shifted his legs, as if bracing for Miss Carberry to bound out another window. Thankfully ground floor windows were less conducive to producing heart murmurs. He eyed her warily and sat down on an armchair. The velvet fabric seemed to scratch him, even though previously he would always have termed the fabric opulent.

"How nice to see you, Miss Carberry," he said. "I—er—haven't seen you since the marquess's house party."

Miss Carberry raised her eyebrows, and he gave her a mild smile, calculated not to inspire musings on the past night. He refused to admit to anyone that he'd seen her in his bedroom the night before. Some things should remain secrets.

"And I brought my grandmother," she said brightly.

"Ah." He turned his attention to the woman beside her. "Not your mother."

Miss Carberry shook her head firmly.

Jasper had fought in the war and he tended to assign dangerous qualities to people lighting cannons and thrusting bayonets. Miss Carberry's grandmother might not be holding a match, much less have a cannon before her, but he still inched into his armchair.

"My grandmother is my father's mother," Miss Carberry said.

"Ah..." Jasper's shoulders eased. "So, she's entirely unrelated to your mother."

"Precisely."

Jasper nodded rapidly. "Good, good."

This day hadn't taken a dreadful turn after all. It had veered so abruptly last night to the side of all things atrocious that Jasper hadn't been certain whether his luck had abruptly ended and the whole world would forever be just a bit worse and that he would always be able to point to the exact day, the exact moment, in which everything good had ended, never to be recovered.

Jasper sprang up, informed Powell to tell the housekeeper to bring tea, then settled back into his armchair.

"The weather is nice today, is it not?" Jasper asked brightly.

"Unlikely to produce mud," Miss Carberry said amiably. "I have a proposition for you."

"A proposition?"

"Indeed?" Despite his best intentions, his voice trembled. Hopefully she did not mean the marital sort.

She nodded. "I need to find a husband."

"That was clear from your mother's behavior," he remarked.

Her cheeks pinkened, but she didn't avert her gaze and she didn't make an excuse to leave.

"Did you have a particular husband in mind?" his voice squeaked, and he coughed.

The last thing he desired was for her to say that he made the ideal husband. It wouldn't be an unusual statement. Plenty of matchmaking mamas had told him the same thing, usually before stating how their daughters were uniquely equipped to manage Jasper's vast estates—as if he were incapable of hiring good estate managers and housekeepers, and as if he were completely flummoxed by the prospect of choosing a dinner menu or color scheme.

If Jasper could battle Bonaparte's army, he could certainly tackle a menu, no matter how much it might shock the women of the *ton*.

"It's not you," Miss Carberry said, clearly reading his mind.

"Good," he said, and her cheeks pinkened in that delightful manner again.

He sighed. Perhaps it was ungentlemanly to appear utterly horrified at the thought of marrying her.

"I mean," he corrected, "I have no desire to marry anyone."

"You don't need to," she said.

He nodded. "Very astute."

The housekeeper came with the tea, and they were silent. He wasn't going to give the housekeeper any fodder for marital speculations. She had a dreadful habit of having her eyes mist at the prospect of him marrying. There were reasons why most people didn't have servants who remembered one in leading strings.

Instead, he relaxed into the wingchair and scrutinized Miss Carberry. He'd seen her before, of course, but she never drew attention to herself. At Hugh's house party, the other women had excelled at conversation, and he'd talked with them about the weather, high society gossip, and the virtues of good manners.

He'd had no such conversations with Miss Carberry. She'd talked rarely, and when she did, she had a horrible habit of talking about the wrong thing. She even sounded different from the other women, even if there was something appealing about the Scottish lilts of her accent. Miss Carberry had once entered into an entire monologue about the supposed marvels of earthworms at his friend's house party. There was never a good time to talk about earthworms, but dinner was the very worst time to introduce the conversation. Frankly, Jasper was quite content to pretend that earthworms did not exist. The thought seemed to create a much more pleasant world, no matter what Miss Carberry might think.

"I was hoping—" Miss Carberry paused, and her face pinkened. She then inhaled and focused her gaze on her tea.

Miss Carberry's grandmother smiled benignly, and Miss Carberry stirred her tea. A clanging noise sounded as her spoon hit the porcelain cup.

She was nervous.

Most likely Miss Carberry desired a favor. Money, perhaps, as an acknowledgment that she'd saved him from a dreadful fate. Perhaps she'd contemplated the potential benefits of being a duchess.

Well, he could compensate her. Whatever she wanted. He was damned grateful. Besides, he had plenty of coin. Coin was not the issue.

Finally, Miss Carberry raised her gaze. "I was hoping you might dance with me."

"Dance?" Jasper lurched his eyebrows upward and glanced toward the empty space beside the chaises. "N-Now?"

"No, no," Miss Carberry said quickly. "At a ball. Where people might see us. In fact, if you were to give the impression you enjoyed dancing with me, it is possible other men might—"

"—desire to dance with you?" Jasper finished.

She widened her eyes, evidently surprised Jasper had come to the conclusion with only minor prompting.

The correct answer was no, obviously.

Jasper had escaped marriage and now he could throw himself into all his normal pleasure-making activities. He certainly didn't want to be thought to be courting a wallflower. A man had a certain reputation to keep up. One wouldn't want to make a sartorial error and accessorize with the wrong style of shoe, and one certainly wouldn't want to be seen with the wrong type of chit.

And yet...

It had been dashed decent of Miss Carberry to not wait in the room and insist they marry. It had been even more decent of her to hide out the window.

She'd risked her entire life.

Jasper had vowed to himself he would grant her anything. He'd been imagining she would desire some sort of financial gift. Most people were quite simple, and were equally enamored in the unwavering, consistent coin.

"I can't do it," he said finally.

"Oh." Miss Carberry's face fell.

Jasper ignored the tinge of guilt that thrummed through him. He rose and paced the wooden floor, moving over the oriental carpet placed underneath the coffee table and chairs.

"It's not a horrible idea," he amended.

"But you won't do it," she said.

He nodded. "Exactly so."

There was an awkward silence in the room, and Miss Carberry's grandmother munched on a sweet. Perhaps the elder Mrs. Carberry thought it likely that Miss Carberry might leave abruptly and had decided to avail herself of Monsieur Parfait's sugar delicacies.

If so, the elder Mrs. Carberry was a wise woman. Monsieur Parfait's delicacies were brilliant.

"The fact is," Jasper continued. "It won't work."

Miss Carberry frowned. He'd thought she might frown, and he continued on, ignoring the instinct that he must make her laugh. Normally he could achieve it quickly by sticking out his tongue or standing on his head. Still, if her mood really matched the downward slope of her lips, there was a chance she might fling the sweets at him.

"The dance might achieve some gossip," he said, "but it won't be enough."

"Because I'm not enough?" her voice wobbled.

"Because we need to find you a good husband," he said.

Her eyebrows darted up.

"I fear a man whose sole attraction in a bride is that a man with means showed interest might make an imperfect husband."

She blinked.

He stretched his shoulders and gave a self-satisfied smile. Suddenly, it was very important that she be pleased. She could have asked for anything, and all she'd wanted was a dance. He imagined having a mother apt to tying up her daughter in strange men's beds might make one have a cautious disposition.

"I have another plan," he said confidently. "A better one."

She raised her eyebrows.

"It is essential you marry quickly. You are quite astute to make that observation." Jasper paced the room, excitement pacing through him. "I will find you a husband. An excellent one."

"Oh?" Miss Carberry picked up her teacup and took a sip.

"All you need," he said, "is a duke."

CHAPTER SIX

"A-A DUKE?" MARGARET sputtered, regretting she'd taken that sip of tea. The hot liquid sloshed through her throat as she spoke, and she coughed.

Concern shown in the duke's gaze.

"I'm afraid I misheard you," she said. "Perhaps I developed a cold on the way home last night."

The concern in his eyes grew.

Dukes weren't supposed to be pleasant people. Dukes were supposed to be vile. Hadn't their ancestors achieved their titles through a combination of battle and a willingness to slash other people's heads off? Hadn't dukes possessed an equal amiableness to socialize with Britain's consistently corrupt leaders, who when there was no war, still found an excuse to kill people?

The Duke of Jevington didn't meet those expectations. After all, he'd been shocked last night, but his face hadn't turned purple, and his fingers hadn't formed fists.

But what he'd said now must have been a mistake. Because it sounded as if—she shook her head. Naturally, he wasn't suggesting *he* should marry her.

Even though he was a duke.

Even though she'd never met any other dukes.

"Excuse me?" she asked finally, because staring dumbly was unlikely to be considered polite.

"I said you need to marry," the duke said patiently.

"And what did you say after that?" Her voice squeaked, and she cleared her throat, though the action did not relieve the sudden tightness in her chest.

His lips spread into their customary smile. The man was a paragon for politeness.

Perhaps the duke was accustomed to women being astounded in his presence, though it wasn't his exquisite symmetrical features, his tallness and his manner of fitting his attire with a skill normally reserved for mannequins, that left her on edge: it was his words.

"I said I would help you," he said gently, as if he were a tutor and she were a comprehension-challenged pupil.

She nodded.

"And then I said I would find you a duke."

Her eyes widened. The man had said the word again.

He grinned, clearly pleased with himself. "A duke."

She stared at him.

But he'd clearly said duke. *Multiple* times. She'd thought her heart had quickened when she'd seen him before, but now it careened.

Perhaps he was teasing her.

Yet his eyes seemed kind, and she doubted he had any acquaintances hiding behind the chaise whom he wanted to make laugh.

Suddenly, the room seemed devoid of air, despite the generous sizes of the windows and ample square footage.

The man was so close.

Close enough to sweep her in his arms.

Close enough for their lips to meet.

Close enough...

She stepped away hastily, bumping into a sideboard. The wooden edge poked her leg, and an oriental vase wobbled precariously, sending flower petals tumbling.

He grasped her elbow with one hand, and energy thrummed through her body.

"I-I don't understand," she stammered finally, not wanting to glance at her grandmother, lest even her expression be filled with mirth.

Normally, Margaret understood things.

It was one of her good qualities.

One of her *few* good qualities.

"I thought your mother would prefer a duke. Unless, you don't like dukes?" A hurt expression flitted on his face.

"I don't abhor dukes."

"Truly?"

"Truly."

He beamed, and the world seemed good again.

"But there's one problem," she said. "How do you expect a duke to marry me? I hope you're not planning to take inspiration from my mother and plan on sneaking me into various residences belonging to your ducal friends and tie me up to their bedposts."

His lips twitched. "I have no attention of putting your wrists through that."

"Oh."

He took her hands, then traced her wrists. "Are you still in pain?"

Margaret shook her head. "Pain is the last thing I'm thinking of."

For some reason Grandmother Agatha laughed from her position on the chaise, but she quickly busied herself by pouring more tea.

The duke dropped her hands slowly, as if remembering that touching them ranged on the improper. "They'll fall in love with you."

Margaret's eyes widened. The man must be mad.

"A love match is the easiest solution to your lack of noble blood," he said. "Don't you agree?"

She nodded, still astounded. "But there are only seven unmarried dukes in Britain."

"And one of them is a nonagenarian," he said. "Not an ideal match, even for your mother. But the others are sterling candidates."

"One of them is betrothed to my friend."

"You're acquainted with Lady Juliet?"

She nodded, still feeling a tinge of regret she hadn't been able to see her at the ball. What must Juliet and Genevieve think of her absence? When they'd been in finishing school, Juliet had urged them to start a *Duke Hunters Club*. Juliet had been the only one to succeed. She'd also been the only one to attempt it.

Jasper scrunched his forehead. "I hadn't realized they were still..."

Margaret looked at him sharply, and his cheeks grew ruddy.

"Well, I haven't seen him in a long time."

"He does favor the Lake District," Margaret said.

The duke nodded. "I suspected something might have happened between them, but clearly he just wants to spend time at his estate."

"Estates are difficult to manage," Margaret said, before remembering the duke was well acquainted with that fact and was managing from afar.

"Quite. No doubt he wants to make certain it's perfect before the wedding."

Margaret's shoulders eased. "No doubt."

"And—er—they will soon have a lifetime together. The others are still eligible."

"How precisely do you mean for one of them to propose?" Margaret asked. "I can't even get into Almack's."

"Few people can get into Almack's. The proprietresses don't want everyone to know about the horribleness of their cake." He shuddered, and she found herself smiling.

"I don't think that secret is very well hidden."

"To taste it is another thing," the duke said.

"Quite unlike your sweets," Grandmother Agatha interjected.

"Ah, that is the work of Chef Parfait."

"Is that his true surname?" Margaret asked.

Jasper scrunched up his forehead, giving him the appearance of a boy attempting to divide fractions for the first time. "You know... I never asked. But I find it describes him admirably. As for finding a husband for you... I will have a house party. These things normally take care of themselves after that."

"Oh?"

"My estate is quite conducive to romance," he said modestly.

"So, you'll have a whole house party to find me a husband?"

"Naturally."

The duke paced the room. Energy wafted through him, and his strides were longer than necessary for the room.

"Thankfully, it's the end of the season, and everyone is still in town. I'll invite them to my Dorset residence for a long weekend." He turned to her abruptly. "Does that work for you?"

"Did you say Dorset?" she squeaked.

He nodded. "Unless you would prefer my Surrey estate?"

"Not necessarily. Where in Dorset is your estate?"

"By the coast," he said. "So rather a farther drive. But it's quite pretty. Appropriate for all this warm weather."

Heavens.

Dorset was where all those wonderful fossils had been discovered.

Fossils that seemed to be of huge, wingless reptiles.

Incredible fossils.

Margaret knew she should refuse. And yet— For a blissful moment she imagined wandering the Dorset coast, and her heartbeat raced.

"Are you quite well?" the duke asked.

"My granddaughter has read about Dorset," Grandmother Agatha said.

"Good things, I hope?" the duke's eyes glimmered.

Margaret's cheeks warmed, but she managed to nod.

"Well then." The duke shot her another grin, the type that managed to send an ache through her heart as surely as if he'd stabbed it with a bow. "It's decided. Is three weeks from now fine?"

"My schedule is free," she said faintly.

"Excellent." The duke ushered her from the townhouse. The man seemed to bounce when he walked. She'd never met anyone like him.

He can't mean it.

He rubbed his hands together. "It will be jolly good to see everyone together."

"I'm glad," she said.

She'd come to see him, but she lacked any control in the conversation. The point hadn't been for him to crown himself matchmaker: she'd simply asked him to dance with her at a single ball.

Nervousness fluttered through her. Spending a long weekend with a group of dukes seemed a particularly unrelaxing way to while about the time. Dukes were most likely to be well versed in the intricacies in etiquette, a trait she did not share.

She refrained from speaking. Speaking might lead her to tell him that his plan was absurd. People didn't simply suggest she married a duke. Dukes were the very pinnacle of society. They outranked marquesses, earls, viscounts and barons. And she was Margaret Carberry. When a duke married, he would select someone similar to himself: someone with a title, someone whom people extolled for their skills in water coloring, crocheting and beauty maintenance.

The duke beamed at her. There was something so appealing in his grin that she didn't want to say that his idea was in any manner lacking.

Grandmother Agatha rose. She'd seemed focused on her tea, but perhaps she'd been following the conversation. "It's time for us to go. We have many engagements."

Margaret's eyebrows rose, but Grandmother Agatha smiled innocently at the duke.

"Ah, naturally." The duke scratched the back of his neck absent-mindedly. "Then I will see you in Dorset."

"In Dorset," Margaret squeaked.

Grandmother Agatha took Margaret's arm, and they left the townhouse. The carriage was waiting for them outside, and she helped her grandmother into it.

"What a nice young man," Grandmother Agatha said.

"Yes," Margaret agreed. "Though I don't think he will truly invite me to his castle."

"He did say he would, my dear. Honor is important to the right sort of man, and the duke *is* the right sort of man."

Margaret and Grandmother soon returned to the townhouse. Margaret nodded to the butler, hoping not to enter into conversation. The sooner she could slink upstairs the better. Margaret hadn't seen her mother since last night and she had no desire to quicken that questionable pleasure.

Footsteps sounded from the drawing room, and Margaret braced herself.

"You've returned!" Mama said.

"Yes."

"I've been besieged with worry." Mama clasped her hands together, resembling a Renaissance pieta painting.

Margaret raised her eyebrows, and Mama's cheeks pinkened. She turned around. "Well—you shouldn't have left with your grandmother."

"We just returned from a drive," Grandmother Agatha said.

Margaret and Mama both turned to her, but Grandmother Agatha nodded firmly. "To a lovely section of London."

Grandmother Agatha's expression exuded innocence. White curls had a habit of imbuing one with an angelic appearance, as if one had stepped from a gossamer cloud, and Grandmother's head was covered with them.

"Well." Mama scrunched her thin lips. "I suppose that isn't unreasonable."

"Er—yes. I should go to my room," Margaret squeaked, hastening up the steps.

Mama hadn't spoken of last night's adventures, and Margaret had no desire to raise the subject. She suspected her behavior had made her opinion clear.

Margaret entered her bedroom and headed for her bookcase. She perused her trusty collection of books. She needed something to distract herself. She moved her hand across the familiar spines. Even reading about the classification of birds seemed of less immediate interest than normal.

She needed something to distract herself from memories of the duke's chiseled face and of his easy affability, something to make her no longer think of the energy that had swirled through her when he'd caught her from falling, and something to make his sonorous tenor voice no longer ring in her thoughts.

Margaret selected her favorite book anyway and turned the pages. Birds flickered over the page.

"Darling!" Mama's voice boomed through the townhouse with a force most opera singers would envy. "You have an invitation."

Margaret placed her book down, and her heartbeat quickened. She recalled the duke's conversation. Was this invitation to visit him?

The thought was absurd. The duke might have convinced himself when she was there that he would assist her in acquiring a husband, but surely, at some point, wouldn't he have changed his mind?

"Margaret!" Mama's voice thundered. "It's from the duke."

"The duke?" Papa's voice sounded from the library.

There were few things that caused Margaret's father to remove his gaze from his business ledgers.

Apparently, this invitation was one of them.

Margaret closed her book, left her room and hurried down the corridor. She moved swiftly. This place was so new, it lacked the abundance of sideboards, vases, and oriental carpets that dotted the townhouses of the *ton*. Since the English forbade Scottish from wearing tartan, Margaret's mother had dutifully tossed out all reminders of Scotland from the house. Her sacrifice proved unnecessary: the English now embraced everything Scottish, lauding Sir Walter Scott's poetry with particular glee. No ancestors stared at her from gilt-framed portraits. Papa was the first Carberry to have made the name significant.

Mama continued to wail, and Margaret sprinted down the steps. The butler shot her a disapproving look, and Margaret slowed her pace.

No doubt the butler's past employers had not raced about the townhouse.

No doubt the butler's past employers had also refrained themselves from using every volume level when they spoke.

Margaret rounded the corner and found her mother in the drawing room. Part of a scarlet seal lay on the table, as if Mama had hastily opened the letter clutched in her hand.

"The man must have been so overcome by the sight of you," Margaret's mother exclaimed. "He has invited you to his castle for the weekend. Imagine that!"

Margaret sat on a chaise as her father entered the room. Lily strode beside him, wagging her tail, as if excited at the unexpected excursion from the library to the drawing room. Most days Lily lay curled at Papa's feet.

"I'm certain I'm not invited there alone," Margaret said.

Mama beamed but scanned the letter, as if to ascertain its contents. "Oh, indeed! I am invited. As is your dear father and—" she frowned, "your grandmother. Most curious."

"Lily must come too," Papa announced.

At the sound of her name, Lily rose. Sunbeams shone through the lace curtains, and Lily's short white coat gleamed. Nothing else about Lily was diminutive.

Mama dropped the invitation, then hastily picked it up. "Not Lily."

"Nonsense. A castle will suit her admirably."

"But Lily is so..."

Papa gave Mama a confrontational glance, and she hesitated.

"Why, she's large," Mama said, her voice wobbling.

"I cannot come without Lily." Papa declared and petted Lily.

"Then your daughter cannot be married. For if you do not attend, how can the duke be reassured of the pleasantness of your nature?"

"I am certain the duke has no interest in my nature," Papa said. "He is a young man. He has other concerns. Shooting and mountain climbing and whist and such."

"But if you bring Lily," Mama said, "then how can the duke be charmed?"

"Lily is *most* charming," Papa said.

Mama glanced at Lily skeptically.

"Besides, *we're* visiting him," Papa continued. "He should be charming us. It's quite dastardly to not be charming after urging us to make a lengthy journey."

"His castle is in Dorset. I would hardly describe that as a long journey. We return to Scotland each year. *That* is a long journey."

Papa nodded. Even Margaret nodded, but her heart tightened oddly. Her parents didn't know who the other guests would be. The trip would be filled with all manner of potential mortifications. Margaret would far rather stay here and occupy herself with her books on ornithology. The only consolation was that she would be in the countryside and might be able to explore the coast.

"Perhaps he will even desire to invest in my company," Papa mused, a content expression on his face.

"You mustn't conduct any business," Margaret said hastily.

"I quite agree." Mama rose. "Now you must come with me."

"Where?"

"To prepare." Mama grasped Margaret's hand and yanked her up. "You must look your very best this weekend. This is a moment for Madame Abrial."

Margaret's heart sank.

Madame Abrial was the modiste most *en vogue* with the *ton*. Unfortunately, Margaret abhorred visiting her shop. For one so lauded, Madame Abrial seemed to take pleasure in expressing doubt about her ability to make Margaret look respectable, emphasizing that her magic had limitations.

"Must we?" Margaret pleaded.

Mama gave her a stern stare, and for a horrible moment, Margaret remembered Mama tying her to the duke's bedposts. Perhaps that attempt had been unsuccessful, but Margaret had no desire to test the limits of Mama's creativity.

"Very well," Margaret said.

Mama beamed. Soon, Margaret exited the townhouse for the second time today, though this time, Mama directed the driver on where to go.

The carriage swept through London. The streets became more crowded, and finally the carriage halted before a shop.

Margaret followed her mother into Madame Abrial's store. A dress shop was a poor use of the space's limited size. Margaret squeezed past gowns, toward the large glass display cases for fabric. Though this was a surprisingly sunny day in January, the light that had beamed into the street, unthwarted by London's fog, was evidently not able to pierce through Madame Abrial's crowded display case.

A few women, younger than her, turned in her direction. Perhaps they would debut next season. They returned soon to their perusal of ribbons and lace.

"What has Madame Abrial's become?" One of the women shook her head.

Margaret stiffened.

The woman directed her attention to Margaret. "They're bringing in the riff raff."

Her companion giggled.

Margaret doubted either woman had given much thought to physics before, but they must know Margaret could hear them. Surely, they knew sound didn't stop traveling simply because one said something unpleasant.

The woman raised her chin and glanced again at Margaret. There was a cruel icy look in her eyes.

She knew Margaret could hear.

And she didn't care.

This wasn't the first time Margaret had been confronted with this situation. Her mother was always adamant that Margaret should be in the best places, and the people in the best places were baffled by her presence.

Margaret didn't blame them.

Her ancestors hadn't liked it when the English had come north either, and it would be foolish to assume the reverse was true. She felt like a foreign invader, but unlike them she wasn't carrying a pistol.

She was simply Margaret, in clothes that were a trifle too tight to be becoming—

a symbol of her mother's always optimistic hope she would become slimmer—and in a color that was never quite right, no matter how much her mother studied *Matchmaking for Wallflowers* and other journals for fashion advice.

Margaret's mother's face had grown paler, and her lips were tight.

She heard.

"Perhaps we can return another time," Margaret suggested, keeping her voice low.

Mama sniffed. "Nonsense."

Mama hadn't grown up with money. Papa's sudden success had been a surprise to everyone, but Mama struggled valiantly to give Margaret the same options she would have had, if Papa had come from a wealthy family.

Margaret felt the eyes of the other people on her, and stiffened. She moved her hands jerkily over the fabric, struggling to appear to ignore them. Her happiness at receiving the invitation vanished.

Nothing much had changed, and nothing would change after she visited the duke.

Another woman might take advantage of the opportunity. Her friend Emma had managed to land a marquess even though she'd had no desire to do so and had given every indication of finding the marquess's attention inconvenient. But then, Emma was beautiful, and life for her would always be different.

Margaret sighed.

She needed to remember that even if she had received an invitation to visit the duke's home, nothing truly had changed.

CHAPTER SEVEN

JASPER'S MOOD WAS BUOYED: Miss Carberry was alive. Her limbs were intact, and no scratches marred her delicate skin. He sipped his tea and stretched his feet onto his ottoman. His invitation to the Carberry family was sent out, and given his groom's efficiency, her family had probably already explained over its contents.

In truth, organizing the house party was an easier feat than he'd allowed Miss Carberry to believe. These men were his friends, and he'd already arranged to have them visit his castle in Dorset to mark the end of the season.

Sebastian, the Duke of Sandridge, was normally found on the coast in Cornwall. Sandridge spent far too much time on the water. Reginald, the Duke of Hammett, was often partaking in boxing competitions, which at least had the advantage of being on land, even if his bruises appeared uncomfortable. Lucas, the Duke of Ainsworth, was normally happily ensconced in Oxford, as if reluctant to abandon any research books, no matter how obscure. Colin, the Duke of Brightling, was content to dance at balls.

Miss Carberry had seemed so astonished at his ability to plan the house party that he'd hardly wanted to dampen her wonder. Most people didn't look at him with that sense of awe. Curiosity, perhaps. Envy, often. And some people did have a glazed look to their eyes that made him think they found his regular features appealing.

No, Miss Carberry was a damsel in distress, and though he was not a knight—he would do his best to assist her.

He'd be happy to do so.

It had occurred to Jasper that he would not mind being in Miss Carberry's company for longer. She would be quite suitable as a wife of one of his friends. She was intelligent, but more importantly, she was kind. And though he'd dismissed her when they'd first met, she had a certain attractiveness. Her curves for instance were most appealing. He'd considered her frumpy, but perhaps she simply required clothes that fit properly. Today's fashions weren't equipped at displaying the sumptuous curve of her bosom, matched only by the curve of her hips.

The manner in which she'd laid in his bed, her back arched as she strained against her constraints... His chest tightened at the memory.

No, he'd been wrong to dismiss her.

His friends would be wrong if they did as well.

Jasper removed a sheet of paper and placed it on his book. He scrambled for an inkwell and quill, then began to write a list. Most people favored desks, thinking that writing should be done at proper places, but Jasper was eager to make every moment perfect. Sitting in a leather armchair with his feet up and a pleasant view of Grosvenor Square before him was far preferable to sitting at a desk, even if he risked ink splattering over his trousers.

This house party needed to be marvelous. His friends prided themselves on their unmarried state, even if they complained on occasion of languor.

He frowned. Was marriage the sort of thing that banished boredom? Perhaps. For a moment he allowed himself to imagine a marriage. A family. *Happiness.*

He shook his head. No doubt marriage had its advantages, but he'd long ago vowed to not partake in it.

Happiness could be taken away if he depended on it from others. It was far better to find happiness himself and spread it from time to time to his friends and acquaintances. He didn't want to be dependent on anyone else.

Other people might die.

His family had.

Why create a new one if it just brought risks of pain?

Jasper was happy now. Everyone knew it.

He pushed the thought of marriage away. He rarely succumbed to such sentimentality. Or at least, he attempted to rarely succumb to such drivel. Ever since Hugh had married, he'd been thinking more about the institution.

Romance would need to be summoned more naturally. He tapped his quill thoughtfully against his paper. Ink spurted out, and he remembered that writing, not tapping, was the appropriate activity for a quill.

Romance.

1. Music - Violinists are best

2. Flowers - Preference for Roses

3. Fires in Fireplaces

He frowned at the latter. He didn't like to create more work for his servants, so perhaps the fires could be contained to the main halls. This was summer after all. No one should be cold.

He had the impression the list should be longer. It must take more to become married. He blotted his quill, then smiled as more ideas flitted into his mind.

4. *Poetry books*

5. *Long walks at sunset.*

He nodded at the last one. That was it. He must remember not to have Miss Carberry miss sunset.

He set down his quill and removed his gaze from the paper. The house party would proceed perfectly.

READING WAS AN ABSOLUTE impossibility.

Even if Margaret had not been distracted by thoughts of the upcoming house party, she would have been distracted by the sounds thundering through the townhouse. The place had seemed spacious before, but it could not obscure the sounds of Mama barking orders to the servants and urging them to pack each and every item of clothing.

Fortunately, Margaret had somewhere else to be and she pulled her mother aside.

"I'm going to visit Daisy," Margaret said.

Mama sniffed. "Wouldn't it be a better use of your time to spend time with someone who actually is part of society?"

"Daisy's father is a baron, and Papa has no title."

"That might be." Mama shifted her legs, "but you cannot call her *within* society. You attend more events than she does."

"I am not in a chair," Margaret said.

"You do understand." Relief passed over Mama's face, even though that was not the emotion Margaret desired to summon. "I do wish you would spend more time with Lady Juliet. She is engaged to a duke."

Margaret smiled tightly. "I am aware."

"Perhaps you should invite her to the house party," Mama mused. "It would be good for the duke to see you already cavorting with duchesses."

"She's not a duchess yet."

"She will be," Mama breathed, and her eyes shimmered in an odd manner that made Margaret avert her eyes.

"Well, I am going to visit Daisy, just as I do every Tuesday afternoon," Margaret said. "I am certain Percy is already preparing the carriage."

Mama sighed resignedly. "I suppose there will be other people you can see as well."

Margaret did not bother to answer. She was hardly going to imply that the purpose of seeing Daisy was so she might spend time with other people. She certainly wasn't going to mention that Lady Juliet would probably be present. Margaret would have gone to see Daisy by herself, just as she had done the other night.

Instead, she turned and left.

The carriage was indeed prepared, and after putting on a light pelisse and her favorite lace gloves, she soon was on her way toward Mayfair. Normally the sight of Londoners going about their business transfixed her, but now her mind returned to her strange meeting with the duke.

She'd expected him to scoff at Daisy's suggestion. Technically, he had scoffed at her suggestion, but she doubted Daisy would be troubled at the alternative he'd presented.

Margaret arrived and strode toward the door, striving to not recollect her late arrival a few days prior. She inhaled, grasped hold of the door knocker and waited for the door to finally swing open.

"Good afternoon, Miss Carberry." The butler scrutinized her dubiously, no doubt recollecting her late arrival before.

She forced herself to hold up her chin. "I have arrived for tea."

"Miss Holloway and her friends are in the drawing room, Miss Carberry," the butler said.

"Thank you." Margaret hastened toward the room. The sound of her friends' laughter would have been ample indication of their location, even if she hadn't visited often before.

Margaret greeted her friends. An appealing tower brimming with afternoon tea delights sat before them, and Margaret took her customary seat on the chaise between Juliet and Genevieve. Daisy soon poured tea for Margaret, and Portia passed it to her along with a scrumptious apple-flavored sweet.

"You came!" Daisy beamed at her. "I thought you might have been tired from the other night."

"I was a late-night visitor," Margaret explained to the others.

"She came all by herself." Daisy flung her arms. "In a tattered and torn gown. It was *most* dramatic. Poor Jameson has still not recovered. And we're still finding rosettes."

The other women looked at Margaret curiously. They weren't the sort of women to wander about London by themselves. Few women were.

Margaret quickly told them the story. Their eyes widened at appropriate moments, and they let out comforting sighs at others.

"I told Margaret she should ask the duke to dance with her at the next ball to help her find a husband," Daisy said, and the others laughed.

"I would love to see that," Genevieve squealed.

"As the founder of the *Duke Hunters Club*, I admire that suggestion." Juliet gave a regal smile befitting of a woman confident of her betrothal. Her deep burgundy hair gleamed as if it were a crown.

"I thought you would," Daisy said with obvious pride.

"I asked him," Margaret said.

The others stared, but Daisy leaned forward, her eyes shining. "You mean you went to visit him? By *yourself*?"

"Perhaps she thought he would be more likely to say yes if she brought her mother," Portia said.

"By giving him a heart attack." Genevieve turned quickly to Margaret. "Not to be disrespectful."

"I took my grandmother."

Daisy sent her an approving nod. "An excellent move. Shows him how long you can live and how he definitely doesn't want to keep you about as a spinster."

"What did he say?" Juliet breathed.

"Well." Margaret shifted in her seat. Suddenly the room was very hot, and she placed her tea down.

"He must have dismissed her." Genevieve's eyes welled in sympathy. "I'm so sorry, dear."

"No sympathy necessary," Margaret said.

"What exactly did he say?" Juliet asked. "Perhaps we can rectify it."

Daisy nodded gamely. "All of us are here this time. We'll think of something. You needn't worry."

"Well." Margaret picked up her teacup and took a long sip. Finally, she put down her teacup. "I'm going to the Duke of Jevington's estate for a house party."

Her friends blinked. Some of them raised their eyebrows, while others dropped their mouths open.

None of them managed to not appear flabbergasted.

"The Duke of Jevington, you said?" Portia asked finally.

Margaret nodded.

"The Duke of Jevington with all the money?"

"And all the good looks," Daisy added.

The others snickered.

"Yes." Margaret's voice squeaked.

"Well." Genevieve's eyes remained wide. "Enjoy yourself."

The advice might be sound but enjoying herself seemed absolutely the last thing she would be doing.

"Look," Margaret said. "There are seven unmarried dukes in England."

Portia raised an eyebrow. "How did you know that?"

"How do you *not* know that?" Juliet shook her head, and her red locks bounced. "Everyone knows that. Besides, one of them is a nonagenarian, and one of them is my betrothed."

"The Duke of Jevington informed me," Margaret said.

Genevieve blinked. "As trivia? Facts of interest?"

"He told me he plans to invite them to the party." Margaret shrugged. "Of course, he was jesting. Naturally."

For a moment she'd allowed herself to believe he would invite a group of dukes, but that had been a momentary lapse. He couldn't have been serious. He couldn't *stay* serious.

The others nodded, but Daisy's eyes glimmered.

"Men are only grown-up little boys," Portia said in a kind manner. "One must remember that. They can be liable to jesting. All that time at school with nothing to do but to tuck frogs underneath one another's pillows."

"Heavens, I hope none of the dukes retain that habit," Margaret said. "Lily can be quite energetic about her disapproval of reptiles."

"Imagine Lily chasing them!" Genevieve exclaimed, and the others squealed and giggled.

"A house party..." Juliet murmured. "How lovely."

Juliet was correct.

It should be lovely.

But Margaret's heart still thrummed a nervous rhythm, and she turned to her friend. "My mother mentioned she wouldn't mind if you joined us. Given your—er—betrothed status."

"There are even more reasons to find a husband," Portia moaned.

Margaret shot a guilty look at her other friends. "I'm sorry. She didn't invite everyone."

"And she shouldn't," Daisy said. "This is a moment for you alone. Does the duke know about the invitation?"

"I doubt his castle is devoid of rooms," Juliet said. "Besides, I should meet the other peers in my future husband's circle."

"I imagine the weekend would be difficult even with the possibility of spending time with dukes," Genevieve said.

There was an awkward silence. No doubt everyone was pondering Margaret's mother and her proclivity toward pushiness.

Even if Juliet came with her, this would still be an uncomfortable house party.

CHAPTER EIGHT

THE FOLLOWING WEEK the grooms piled their trunks onto the carriage, and Margaret, Juliet, Mama, Papa, Grandmother Agatha and Lily squeezed inside. The maid sat with the driver. Papa removed a ledger from his purse and placed it over his lap.

"Please tell me you're not going to work." Mama fluttered her arms.

"I would not want to lie to you, sweetheart," Papa replied.

The carriage jerked to a start. Lily barked, as if to alert everyone on the carriage's ability to move and to introduce new sights and scents with appealing regularity. Finally, she curled up at Margaret's feet.

"Now you must be on your best behavior when you meet the duke," Mama said. "The man is most important."

"I'd like to determine his importance when I meet him," Papa said.

Mama gave a weak laugh. "You know he's important. He's a duke."

"One tends to wonder at a man whose most successful accomplishment happened when he was born."

"I'm not wondering," Mama squealed. "I'm admiring it."

"Yes, you've made your opinion clear. Well done."

Mama scrunched her lips, temporarily bewildered into silence.

Papa leaned back with a pleased expression on his face and winked.

If Papa could control Mama, he could control any boardroom. Papa opened his ledger, Juliet opened a novel, and Margaret opened her ornithology book. Papa shot Margaret an approving glance.

Margaret studied the pages.

Slowly, excitement moved through her. She was going to Dorset. The place where those fascinating fossils had been discovered. Perhaps she might find some herself.

Grandmother Agatha removed her needlework and began to sew.

Mama peeked at Grandmother's embroidery hoop. "Is that Lily?"

Grandmother nodded. "Precisely."

"Then we shall see her more often in the house." Mama's voice trembled. "How—er—marvelous."

Margaret grinned.

Papa may have taken to Lily, but Lily was still her dog. She'd discovered her abandoned as a puppy, and Papa had agreed that she needed to live with them.

The coach made multiple stops to change horses. The publican ushered them into private dining rooms, each varying in degrees of coziness. Margaret attempted to eat, but her stomach felt weak.

Coach travel lacked pleasantness. Mama's speeches on how Margaret might be more seductive and capture the duke did not improve the experience. Papa rolled his eyes on occasion, shooting Margaret a kind smile, but most of his focus was on his ledgers.

They attempted to sleep in public houses by night, in the coach during the day, even if the uncomfortable swaying, rigid seats and crowded compartment rendered the latter difficult. Finally, the landscape shifted, and she could hear the waves.

They were here.

On the coast.

Perhaps she might wander over the same coastline where those large creatures had once wandered. Lily paced the carriage, perhaps sensing her excitement.

Margaret scooted to the side and pulled back the velvet drape. The drape's thickness was practical when sleep was desired, but less so when one wanted to enjoy the view. Finally, a long, wide strip of marvelous azure appeared.

The English Channel.

Margaret's heart quickened, and she moved her gaze from the sparkling waves, their crests glinting like diamonds, to the coastline that curved beside it, adorned with tawny cliffs.

"Margaret! Margaret!" Mama's wail interrupted Margaret's musings, and she jerked her head.

"Look there!" Mama pointed at the other window.

The view from the other window seemed of far less interest. No waves were visible. Yet, when Margaret moved toward the window, a large manor house loomed before them.

Not that manor house was the correct word: it was a castle, in every sense. Juliet gasped, and even Mama was silent as they drove nearer. The building emanated beauty.

The red stone structure loomed over the trees and rolling hills that surrounded the building, contrasting with the azurean heavens. Large windows curved in an appealing manner. This was not the intimidating castles of the middle ages, with battlements for archers to direct arrows at any intruders.

Lily bounded up and began to howl.

"Bad dog," Mama scolded her.

Lily ignored Mama. Sometimes, Margaret wondered whether that quality made Papa like her so much. Instead, Lily jumped up, placed her paws on the window, and stuck her tongue out in a gesture Margaret assumed was of happiness and recognition of the heat, and not due to being unimpressed by the surroundings.

Lily barked as the coach swung onto a path, flanked by magnificent evergreen trees, and she barked as the coach continued past a small lake, containing a tiny, adorable island. Lily barked as the coach moved past a rose garden, and the agreeable scent drifted inside, and she barked as the coach finally slowed.

The carriage stopped, and Margaret inhaled. She smoothed her dress hastily, even though the carriage was cramped, making the most cursory preening an impossibility. Mama had piled the carriage high with trunks so Margaret would have bountiful wardrobe options, but that had only managed to lead to additional creases in her traveling gown. Hopefully the housekeeper could whisk them to their rooms before they met the duke.

The driver and maid exited the top of the carriage, and Margaret waited for her family to exit. Lily panted happily.

The castle had appeared magnificent when viewed through the small window of a moving carriage, the view obscured on occasion by the wobbling curtains and Lily's head.

Now she faced no such obstruction.

The castle soared over her. Birds chirped merrily, as if gleeful they'd found the very nicest place in England to be.

A row of servants stared at them, and Margaret's heart tumbled. Nervousness thrummed unrelentingly through her, but she pasted a wobbly smile on her face. Then the door opened, and a man strolled out.

Unlike the other men who stood before her, this man wore no livery. He was attired in a simple green tailcoat and breeches, attire suited for the country, and yet the man's appearance still caused Margaret's heart to leap. His shoulders were broad, proportionate to his height. He towered over the servants.

"It's the duke," Mama squealed, elbowing Papa.

Lily let out another bark, then dashed toward the duke, dragging Papa, holding onto her lead, after her.

The duke strode forward, and his tousled brown locks glimmered underneath the sunbeams, revealing strands of honey. No doubt sunbeams enjoyed lingering about the castle—and the duke.

JASPER EYED THE NEW arrivals curiously. Mr. and Mrs. Carberry had that disheveled look common after long journeys, but he was most interested in the large, white spotted dog before him.

When Mrs. Carberry had accepted his invitation and told him they would be taking their dog, he'd imagined a daintier creature, with long fluffy ears, curly locks, and tiny legs. This dog varied tremendously.

"I'm sorry," Mrs. Carberry said. "Lily! Come here!"

Lily pushed her snout against his buckskin breeches, and he smiled and bent down and petted her.

Lily was large with small, entirely unfluffy ears, which pointed up. Her coat was short, though her legs extended to a considerable length.

"Lily!" Mrs. Carberry called again in an exasperated tone. "I'm so sorry, Your Grace."

"There's nothing to apologize for," Jasper said lightly. "It is a pleasure to see you again."

"Er—yes," Mrs. Carberry said.

"I see you found your daughter."

"Indeed." Mrs. Carberry shifted her legs, and the gravel crunched beneath her. She gazed at him cautiously, as if she were not entirely certain he was not going to berate her and send her on her way.

Well, she would deserve that.

Miss Carberry, however, did not deserve that.

Though Jasper would not characterize himself as taking pleasure in the discomfort of others, he didn't entirely mind that Mrs. Carberry's face was paler than it had been a moment ago.

He glanced toward the carriage, hoping to spot her, but the groom was busy assisting the elder Mrs. Carberry to the ground, a process made more difficult by her large bonnet and evident desire not to damage it.

Lady Juliet exited the carriage, and Jasper bowed to her. He'd been vaguely aware that Lady Juliet was considered a good catch, a fact of which she seemed equally aware, and he'd been unsurprised when her betrothal had been announced.

Miss Carberry stepped hastily from the carriage, nearly toppling from it. Though her hair was disheveled, and her dress creased, the pretty pinkness of her cheeks was unmistakable. She fluttered long dark eyelashes up and the edges of her lips extended uncertainly.

Lily moved toward her, evidently excited to be rejoined with her even after a short separation, and Miss Carberry petted her.

Jasper's heart warmed, and he dipped into a deep bow. "It is a pleasure to see you again."

"Er—yes." Miss Carberry's voice squeaked, and she curtsied. "Your Grace, please let me present my father, Mr. Carberry."

"An honor," Jasper said. "I've read much about you in *The Times*. What you're doing for job creation in Edinburgh is a revelation."

Mr. Carberry beamed. "I'll be doing it in London soon."

"Please do not bore the duke," Mrs. Carberry admonished.

Building and maintaining a great business empire wasn't something Jasper found tiresome. He leaned toward Mr. Carberry. "We'll talk later."

Mr. Carberry gave a benign smile with the air of a man whose mind was occupied thoroughly elsewhere. Jasper's mind was making no such travels. He nodded to his newest hires, and they approached him quickly.

Finally, Jasper greeted the elder Mrs. Carberry. After they'd both ascertained they were doing well and that the castle was pretty, he led his new guests to the row of servants.

He turned to the Carberry family. "Please, let me introduce you to the other guests. They're in the drawing room. Monsieur Parfait's sweets are proving occupying." He nodded to his chef.

The elder Mrs. Carberry clapped her hands. "I'm an admirer of yours, Monsieur Parfait."

"Oh?" The chef paled, then swept gallantly into a bow. "You have made me most pleased."

"You must share your recipes with me," the elder Mrs. Carberry continued. "Perhaps you can teach me your tricks."

"Ah, I can write something up for your servants before you leave."

"Servants? Ha. You're speaking to a great baker." The elder Mrs. Carberry placed her hands on her waist, and it was suddenly very easy to imagine her showing her disapproval by brandishing a rolling pin.

Mrs. Carberry ran toward her mother-in-law, nearly tripping on her dress.

"It's her hobby. That's all! Hobby," Mrs. Carberry practically shouted at Monsieur Parfait.

The elder Mrs. Carberry frowned. "But—"

"Baking is something people with less money do," Mrs. Carberry reminded her, though unfortunately she did not select a sufficiently low level, for Monsieur Parfait managed to look offended.

"Monsieur Parfait is excellent," Jasper said hastily. "He's one of the few servants who traveled with me from my London townhouse. One doesn't want to be too far removed from him and his culinary expertise. I suspect the servants in the castle are enjoying his presence as well."

"Quite nice," Mr. Carberry said.

Finally, the Carberry family followed Jasper into the castle. Miss Carberry's faint vanilla scent wafted behind him. The scent was appealing, not reminiscent of the cloying floral scents that seemed in fashion. Perfumers seemed to delight in concocting novel formulae, taking glee in combining obscure fragrances that would never be found together in the natural world.

He shook his head. He shouldn't be musing on Miss Carberry's scent, no matter how alluring it was.

His burly new hires strode close at his side, and the tension in his shoulders eased.

CHAPTER NINE

MARGARET FOLLOWED THE Duke of Jevington into a large foyer. Black-and-white tiles gleamed, contrasting with high cerulean walls adorned with ornate molding. Her footsteps echoed in the empty room, as if she weren't truly supposed to be here.

That, at least, was true.

The duke led them with the same air of confidence he always had. His hair curled, revealing a sliver of bare skin between his head and informal cravat. She pulled her gaze from his neck. It would be too easy to linger on the generous width of his shoulders, and the perfect proportions of the rest of his body.

Large men accompanied him. They lacked the formal attire of footmen. Most footmen were young with pleasing visages that made them not an unwelcome sight in dining rooms where every other detail had been carefully mulled over to make it exquisite. Most footmen did not seem as if they'd made it to the advanced age of thirty-five through vigorous battles.

These were no footmen, and Margaret shivered.

They exited the foyer and entered a great room. This room was filled with furniture. Velvet chaise-longues reclined beside red leather armchairs. Margaret would have found the room intimidating even if it were empty.

Unfortunately, it was not empty.

Handsome men sat on the chaises and armchairs. They smiled blandly as Margaret and her family entered the room, then rose.

Margaret's stomach tightened, and the Duke of Jevington turned around. "Friends, these are my guests, Mr. and Mrs. Carberry. They've brought Mr. Carberry's mother, Mrs. Carberry, their delightful daughter, Miss Carberry, and Lady Juliet."

The men smiled toward Juliet. Men were always smiling at Juliet, and she straightened her shoulders.

"I am exhausted from the journey," Juliet confessed. "I shall go on a walk."

"Would you like help?" a dark haired man with blue eyes asked.

"Naturally not. I have been walking for *decades*. Besides, my betrothed would find male company inappropriate. He is the Duke of *Sherwood*." Juliet exited the room with that peculiar feistiness that comes with people equipped with other advantages, and Margaret was alone.

Mrs. Carberry smiled blissfully. "That is my dear daughter's friend. She will soon be a *duchess*."

There was an awkward silence, perhaps as the men contemplated that the Carberries were untitled. Finally, the Duke of Jevington gestured to the man beside him.

"This is the Duke of Sandridge," the Duke of Jevington said. "He lives in Cornwall."

The man did appear as if he were from Cornwall. His sun-kissed hair was a longer length than normal, falling in casual waves. It was easy to imagine him spending his days by the ocean. Even his skin was a golden color, as if he didn't care that the shade was most often found in hard-working farmers and berry-pickers.

"A pleasure." The duke bowed, and Margaret curtsied hastily.

"And this is the Duke of Hammett," the Duke of Jevington said.

Margaret stared at the man before her. The Duke of Hammett had short, dark hair and he towered above her. Even his neck was large.

"And this is the Duke of Ainsworth," the Duke of Jevington said, gesturing to a thinner man. "Next to him is the Duke of Brightling."

The Duke of Brightling flashed her a wide smile, and his blue eyes sparkled, resembling newly polished sapphires. Margaret had heard rumors about the Duke of Brightling's handsomeness, and unlike other rumors, in this case everything was true.

The dukes were all broad-shouldered and imposing, testaments to generations of good health and their ancestors' strategic marriages with beautiful women.

"You're a duke too?" Mama's voice squeaked.

"We are all dukes," the Duke of Brightling said.

"I see." Mama brushed a hand over her brow. "It seems incomprehensible."

"We're all accustomed to the fact," the Duke of Ainsworth said.

"I suppose you would be," Mama said finally.

The dukes nodded at the veracity of the statement. They appeared like statues that one didn't think should be able to move, since they were already so exquisite. The feat of movement seemed a needless addition to such perfection.

Mama turned her head. "Are those men also dukes?"

Margaret followed Mama's gaze.

Two men stood by the curtains. Men, in Margaret's experience, either came with or without muscles. These men belonged to the former category. Their arms swelled, and their bald heads gleamed, devoid of the tousled locks most men of the *ton* favored. Their clothes seemed of lesser quality than the others, as if they were prepared to run through a bramble bush.

"No," the Duke of Jevington said.

The duke's expression appeared distinctly different. His cheeks hadn't had a habit of shifting color before. He had not seemed prone to mortification, but now, as the man's cheeks adopted a ruddy tint, Margaret considered that perhaps the man had simply not had a reason to be embarrassed.

Of the two of them, Margaret had fulfilled the task better. She'd done sufficient embarrassing things for both of them, even if she did not get the charitable rush of joy one might experience after assisting someone with something of actual importance. Instead, she shifted her legs awkwardly.

"They are my guards," the duke said finally. "Vladimir and—er—Boris."

Margaret's mother's eyes darted up.

"I take security very seriously," the duke continued.

"Naturally. You have many important guests," Papa said.

"The guards are tasked with my protection. I would not—er—desire late night intruders."

"I see." This time Mama's cheeks flamed, and Margaret averted her eyes.

"Would you care to see your room?" the duke asked.

Mama hesitated.

"Oh, absolutely." Papa grinned. "I can get some more work in."

"Of course," the duke said. "We provide desks in all our rooms."

Papa rubbed his hands together.

The duke called for his housekeeper, who soon led them through a corridor. This time they headed toward a grand staircase that curved in a magnificent manner. They strode up the steps, and Margaret placed her gloved hand over the thick glossy wooden banister. Floral patterns were carved into the balusters, and for a moment Margaret stared at the incredible sumptuous surroundings inside the building.

"It's quite lovely, isn't it?" the housekeeper murmured.

"Yes," Margaret said.

"We have staircases in Scotland," Mama said quickly. "They are of a similar quality. My daughter is quite accustomed to staircases."

"Of course," the housekeeper said, and Margaret's face heated.

"This way," the housekeeper gestured to her right, and Margaret's parents turned obediently.

This corridor was quiet, but it dazzled with equal vigor to the main reception rooms downstairs. Beauty was distributed equally here, as if it were doing its part to prevent any of the furniture staging a revolution.

The housekeeper opened a door and gestured to Margaret's grandmother. "This is for you." She looked at Margaret. "Your room is next to it."

Margaret stared at a pleasantly decorated jonquil colored room, then followed her parents to another chamber. In another house the bedroom would have been suited for a drawing room. Even though two canopied beds were in the room, the room remained large, as if the architect had intended any eccentric inhabitant to be able to host parties inside.

Green damask silk lined the walls, and a magnificent molding adorned the high ceiling, as if the designer had found it essential to create the ceiling with the utmost splendor, since it was placed at least fifteen feet above the gleaming wooden floor dotted with equally magnificent oriental carpets.

"I suppose this will do," Mama said. Her voice did not display any particular enjoyment of the surroundings, as if to prevent the housekeeper from reporting back that the Carberry family were not accustomed to such finery. Still, Mama did not normally keep her neck reclined at a sharp angle.

Sunbeams entered through long windows that overlooked the grounds, but it wasn't the immaculate gardens that drew Margaret's attention. Beyond the garden lay a sliver of turquoise.

The ocean.

Margaret's heart soared.

"Are we very far from the coast?" Margaret asked the housekeeper.

"The coast?" The housekeeper raised her eyebrows momentarily.

"Why on earth would you ask about that?" Mama asked. "You'll be spending your time here."

Mama knew why Margaret would ask though.

Mama knew about Margaret's delight in the discoveries Mary Anning had made near Lyme Regis.

She simply didn't approve.

The housekeeper gestured toward a dirt road, lined by majestic chestnut trees. "You can reach the coast by following that path."

"Thank you," Margaret said.

"Yes, so kind of you to indulge her," Mama said to the housekeeper, casting a glare in Margaret's direction. "Obviously, our daughter will not venture from the castle. She is perfectly content with everything here."

"Er—yes." The housekeeper's stalwart expression wobbled, and she suddenly appeared far younger.

Lily pattered happily through the room, taking delight in squeezing underneath sideboards and chairs, as if eager to find a hiding place, though the dog was not conducive to being hidden.

"Be good, Lily," Mama admonished.

"Lily is always good," Papa said staunchly, and Lily wagged her tail.

Mama scrunched her lips with the air of a woman who had a great many circumstances to discuss but was valiantly resisting the impulse to share them.

"Oh, these items are only from the seventeenth century," the housekeeper said lightly. "You needn't worry."

"I see," Mama squeaked, her eyes wide.

"Please ring the bell pull if you need anything," the housekeeper said. "The duke has made everything at your disposal. Dinner is at seven. There will be drinks in the drawing room at six, though you are welcome anytime."

After that short speech, the housekeeper hastened from the room.

"Really," Mama said, turning to Margaret. "I hope you're not going to indulge your strange obsession with bones. It's not ladylike. The duke didn't invite you here to have you digging about on the coast. You will be the death of me."

"They're fossils," Margaret said. "And they're most special. They explain how the world used to be."

"It is far more important to know how the world is today," Mama declared. "So far, you have shown no sign of accomplishing even that. Once you master the current world, you can delve into the past. After all, no man wants to hear you pontificate about the wonders of fossils. Men tolerate women discussing fashion and water coloring techniques, because they can dismiss those things as women's interests."

"Now I'm not certain that's true," Papa said. "Seems to me they might be interested in fossils."

"Even worse," Mama said. "Fossils are a topic some of them might think was something they should be able to discuss. Realizing they lack the knowledge to do so, will cause them discomfort. What sort of woman goes about causing men discomfort?"

"You've made your point," Papa said.

"Thank you," Mama said triumphantly and collapsed onto a conveniently located chaise-longue.

Her mother had that odd gleam in her eyes again. The last time Mama's eyes had gleamed in that manner, atrocious things had occurred.

Mama angled her head toward Papa. "They're *all* dukes. Do you not find it odd?"

"Well, Jevington is a duke," Papa said. "It's not entirely unreasonable for him to have invited other dukes."

Mama frowned, and Margaret had the impression that if her mother were a high ranking noble, she would prefer to surround herself with those who would be suitably awed by her position. After all, Mama had enjoyed Scotland and its absence of titled people from the home counties. There, few people had minded that Papa's money was new.

The *ton* though had a distinct preference for pre-nineteenth century coin. Indeed, Margaret was certain any money that was not pre-eighteenth century was deemed suspect in the eyes of the highest rungs of London society, as if it were tainted by poisonous factory smoke.

Margaret's mother and grandmother decided to test the bedding after the exhausting journey.

"I'm going to explore the place with Lily," Papa said.

Lily wagged her tail at the sound of Papa's words.

Her father glanced at Margaret. "Do you want to come with us?"

Margaret wanted to say no. If she went downstairs, she was bound to see other people, and she chewed her bottom lip. "Perhaps I'll just go to my room."

"Of course, you must go," Mama said sternly, and Margaret soon followed Papa down the stairs. Lily wagged her tail, excitedly sniffing each vase they passed.

She scurried along the oriental carpet, leading them at such a brisk pace, that Margaret was almost surprised when they reentered the reception room.

The Duke of Jevington and his friends rose hastily.

Lily greeted the other dukes, and Papa beamed as they bestowed her with compliments.

"Let me give you a tour," the Duke of Jevington said magnanimously. He turned to his burly companions. "You may accompany me."

Margaret gave a tight smile.

"At a distance of ten feet," he told the two men.

The two men nodded in that somber manner that good servants excel at doing, making certain their employer felt entirely comfortable, if only by making certain no request, no matter how odd, ushered their surprise.

Margaret followed the Duke of Jevington. She'd imagined he would want to wander through the garden or the corridors for his tour, but instead he led her to a balcony. He ascertained the curtains were fully open and not at risk of collapse.

He then opened the door, and she stepped onto the balcony. The large glass windows made it clear what they were doing.

"This offers some privacy," the Duke of Jevington explained, flashing a cocky grin. His two companions lingered on the other side of the door.

No doubt they were accustomed to performing more athletic movements when serving as guards. The guards settled down on a chaise. Though their expressions were still appropriately rigid, their shoulders were relaxed.

"Now what do you think of my friends?" the duke asked. "Do you have a favorite yet?"

"I barely know them," Margaret said. "Besides the concept is—" She hesitated.

"Ridiculous?" the duke offered.

Margaret's cheeks flushed. "It wouldn't be polite to say that."

He shrugged lackadaisically. "I don't much care for politeness. The far more important thing is that it would be wrong. I think you would care about correctness." The Duke of Jevington gave her one of his infuriatingly broad smiles. "It will work. *I* planned it."

The duke did not add anything to his statement. It seemed its ducal origin was enough to be coronated with effusive exaltations.

"But why would they want to marry me?" Margaret asked.

"Miss Carberry," the duke said in an explanatory tone. "No man wants to marry. Not unless they've consumed a steady subsidence of the most atrocious poetry." He leaned closer. "The *romantic* sort. I doubt Dante would make a man overly compelled to resist all reason."

Margaret considered his statement.

"Some men, though, have accepted their fates."

"And you're not one of those men," Margaret said, worried whether she'd overstepped this odd outpouring of confidences.

"It's not my fate," the duke said amiably. "Not now at least."

"I thought all men were desperate to have an heir."

"Perhaps ten years ago," the duke admitted. "When the war on the continent was still raging. But I find it rather less likely that some Frenchman will decide to impale me with a bayonet or will aim a cannon at me. My health is excellent. I have no sisters or mother who might be cast from the castle if some beastly second cousins inherit it. In fact, all my second cousins are quite pleasant. Most unromantic."

"Not everything can be a Jane Austen novel," Margaret said.

"Indeed." The Duke of Jevington bowed his head, as if to give appropriate reverence to that wisdom. "And yet, you will find my friends have excellent qualities. Come, let's join them."

Margaret wanted to visit the coast, but perhaps her mother was correct, and the duke would not find her instinct to wander the coast polite.

No matter.

She would do it as soon as she could.

Margaret nodded and followed the duke into the reception room, ignoring the fact she felt removed from everything she knew. The duke's two men plodded after them.

"You'll love my friends," the duke said. "They're all good men. We've been together since school."

"And they all desire marriage?"

He grinned. "I don't think any of them have that wish. But they'll soon discover it."

"How do you know?"

He raised his eyebrows. "Why, they'll spend time with you."

Margaret knew he hadn't meant anything by his comment, but her heart still fluttered.

CHAPTER TEN

THE AFTERNOON PROGRESSED splendidly. Jasper was not surprised. His festivities were consistently successful. The key was to plan sufficiently in advance so one might maintain a jovial demeanor. Sour expressions destroyed elaborate events with disturbing ease.

His friends might have been baffled by the appearance of Miss Carberry and her parents as well as the vanishing Lady Juliet, the latter whom Margaret's mother had seemed compelled to flaunt, but it didn't matter. Not every man shared his quickness of mind. Without doubt Sandridge still mused above the waves off the cliffs of his beloved Cornwall. He remained oblivious that there was someone present who could be his companion in all things coastal, all things in general.

Most likely Sandridge assumed he could get around to heir-making in a few years, but the journey to London from Cornwall was long. If Sandridge married Margaret, he'd spare himself from missing more time on his beloved coast. Given Miss Carberry's discomfort with London seasons, she'd hardly pine about for them. Sandridge would not be subjected to any guilt generated by a lack of good local haberdashers or balls in which one might flaunt one's tasteful ribbon selections.

But then, Miss Carberry would be equally well-suited to any of his other friends. Ainsworth enjoyed books, a hobby

Jasper was certain he shared with Miss Carberry. Hammett could be intimidating, given his love for boxing, but the normal women of the *ton* did not suit him. He imagined Miss Carberry would be much more relaxed about torn shirts, and no one could question Hammett's sweetness. And as for Brightling—well, everyone adored him.

Mr. Carberry was wealthy. The man's only vice seemed to be the passion to procure more, and Jasper hardly thought that ruled Mr. Carberry out as an inappropriate father-in-law.

Indeed, some of his friends were conscious of the costs of running a large estate. Things were rather different in past decades when one could pop over to the continent at one's leisure, nab a few priceless treasures in the name of Britain's most currently favored religion, then spend the next year happily enjoying its profits. In fact, some of the *ton* had profited from the Napoleonic Wars and were known to stare glumly at world maps, pondering which countries might require their governments to be toppled.

A marriage to Miss Carberry would solve those problems. She possessed a sensible air, and she was unlikely to allocate any freshly stabilized funds to the purchase of gilded furniture, construction of new castle wings, or a newfound desire to have a horse win the Derby. Similarly, she was hardly likely to declare herself a patroness of the arts, and decide to fund the lifestyles of the poets and artists most fueled by expensive drink and desirous of vast clothing budgets to express their personalities in an astonishing and never repeating manner. No, Miss Carberry was a reasonable sort of woman. Her name might not have appeared in the various top debutante lists, but that was an obvious oversight: he could not think of a more suitable wife.

For his friends, he amended.

Obviously, Jasper himself was in no rush to procure a duchess. Life was not everlasting, and he'd planned to maintain a dashing bachelorhood until he reached the age of thirty-five. Parties were not yet dull. At least, not *that* dull. When one spent too much time musing, one was apt to muse about strange things. The quality of one's musings was difficult to keep in order, since the chief admirable quality of musing was its unpredictable manner.

He rounded the corner and entered the reception room.

Unfortunately, his friends were absent, and he raked his hand through his hair. "They—er—were here."

Damnation. They couldn't have got far. This was Dorset, after all.

A footman coughed. "I am to inform you that your friends took the liberty of going upstairs to change into more athletic attire."

He blinked.

"They expressed a desire to play cricket."

"Oh." He frowned and cast a guilty glance at Miss Carberry.

"They don't know the true purpose of the house party." Her eyes shimmered and sparkled, and even though she should be berating him for having failed in retaining the prospective husbands for her, she didn't.

He shook his head miserably.

Her dark eyes sparkled, and the light played in an interesting manner on her round cheeks.

"I'm sorry," he said, his voice husky. "We can go find them..."

"I don't want to interrupt anyone's cricket game. I'll see them this evening."

Right.

That was a sensible plan.

"Before sunset," he said.

"Before sunset," she agreed.

"Splendid." He nodded, multiple times. Somehow his head seemed heavy, moving more slowly than customary. He was less certain around her, as if his body were fighting the urge to stand nearer her, to tuck the loose strand of fallen hair behind her ear, and perhaps, just perhaps, to press his lips against her throat, against her ear, against her lips.

THE DUKE STIFFENED and stepped away from her. "I should change as well, then find my friends."

"Naturally."

For some reason the man's face had paled, and his manner had become overly formal and rigid.

Indubitably, he was regretting inviting her. Most likely now that she was standing in daylight and now that he'd met all of her family, he'd realized the impossibility of any match.

A vile taste invaded her mouth, and she swallowed hard.

Perhaps the duke *had* told his friends he saw her as a potential wife for them. Perhaps they'd disappeared because they'd found her unappealing.

"Goodbye," she said hastily.

"Er—yes." He avoided eye contact with her, seeming to find his shoes more interesting than her face. "Well, this place is at your disposal. There's a library at the other end of the corridor."

"Splendid," she squeaked.

She strode hastily away, before she remembered she would prefer to visit the coast.

Still, perhaps she could visit the library. Her mother hadn't allowed Margaret to take any books with her, seeing them as a poor use of the coach's limited space.

Margaret wandered through the corridor. Heavy Tudor furniture that looked like they could withstand anything dotted the hallway. Margaret had never taken much interest in furniture, merely appreciating those that fulfilled their practical functions, but these pieces could be considered art. Gilt frames sparkled and shimmered and shone, even in the waning afternoon light.

Corridor walking shouldn't be a cause for nervousness. Yet everything was so immaculate, that even though the duke had assured her to feel at home, her spine prickled, as if she might suddenly veer into one of the delicate oriental vases perched on the sideboards and smash it onto the floor.

She peeked inside an open door. Books stretched to the top of the high ceiling. Their leather bindings gleamed, like rows of rubies. Stained-glass windows sprinkled jeweled-colored light over the room, and she stepped inside.

She craned her head, admiring the library in all its glory. Though they'd taken their books when they'd moved from Scotland, her family's collection remained meager: clearly, it took generations to build a collection like this. Wood paneled the ceiling, lending the room warmth.

The mezzanine seemed particularly tempting, and this library deserved to be seen from all angles. She ascended the narrow staircase to the mezzanine. The view met all her expectations: leather-bound tomes gleamed under the light spilling from the stained-glass windows, and their gold titles sparkled.

Margaret brushed her fingers tentatively over them. After perusing the collection, she selected three books, one for each day of her stay, and proceeded down the steps.

Three books might be an excessive number, but she wasn't certain if she could sneak in here easily again. Her mother wouldn't be exhausted from travel every day.

"Excuse me!" A voice startled her, and she jumped, remembering to tighten her grip around her books.

Unfortunately, she did not remember she was on a staircase, and her feet slid.

And slid.

And slid.

The world tilted, and though she'd admired the ceiling when she'd entered the library, she'd hardly required such a rapid view.

Her bottom crashed against the step, and she tumbled downward, her bottom slamming against each additional step in rapid motion.

Finally, her descent ended, and she stared at the ceiling.

It was coffered and sensational, just like everything else.

She felt exceptionally out of place.

Her sentiment was not eased by the sound of footsteps padding toward her at a quick speed.

"Miss? Miss?" a male voice asked.

Margaret sighed and braced herself for inspection by some passing footman, but when she lifted her head, she didn't see a man in uniform. She saw a man who could not be much older than herself in a tweed coat. Leather pads covered his elbows, and he raised his eye monocle.

"Heavens," the man said, and she noted approvingly the selection of a mild exclamation. "Are you quite well? That *was* a tumble."

"Er—yes." Margaret's face heated.

"Let me—er—help you." The man extended his hand, and she gripped cold skin.

She scrambled up quickly, managing to not drop the books.

"I'm afraid I startled you," the man apologized.

"No, no." She shook her head politely. "I shouldn't have been startled. This is a library after all. It is bound to have people."

Now that she was standing, she could properly scrutinize him.

"I am Mr. Octavius Owens. It is a pleasure to meet you."

"I am Miss Margaret Carberry."

"Ah." The man's face did not flicker at recognition at her surname, but he dipped into a polite bow, flashing rounded cheeks and a fringe that seemed too long for his forehead. "It is a pleasure to make your acquaintance."

"Thank you."

He glanced at her books. "You read."

"Indeed."

"A sensible occupation in a young woman like yourself. Though might I suggest you read some botany books?"

"You are fond of the subject?"

"Most. Learning about the natural world is important. After all, it is the world we live in."

She nodded politely.

"*Gulliver's Travels* is a work of fantasy. One might worry that a young lady like yourself might confuse it with reality. I am afraid these authors are most mischievous."

"Mr. Owens, I am not under the impression that giants and flying islands exist."

He lifted his brows. "It is not your first encounter with Swift?"

"Indeed not. Reading is one of my favorite occupations."

"Ah. Most remarkable." Mr. Owens gave her an approving smile and adjusted his eye monocle.

She beamed. She'd made this grumpy man smile.

Unlike the assortment of strapping dukes in the drawing room, this man was not intimidating. His height could not be likened to towers and mountains. In fact, his height mirrored hers. His cravat was tied simply, without the flourish of a man who'd delegated the task to his valet.

"What brings you to this manor house, Miss Carberry?" Mr. Owens asked.

"I am visiting the Duke of Jevington with my parents."

"Ah. Then you are not related to a duke."

Margaret shook her head.

"Few people are I suppose."

"And what brings you here?" Margaret asked, remembering it was polite to carry a conversation, always pressing for new things.

"Ah." The man beamed. "I am here with the Duke of Ainsworth. I work with him on scientific research. It's all *quite* important."

"Oh," she breathed. "You mean you're a *scientist?*"

He gave a lackadaisical shrug. "I'm doing my bit to advance knowledge."

"How lovely," Margaret said, still scrutinizing whether the man's chest had been smaller before. He certainly hadn't been grinning to quite that extent, though she supposed she was unfamiliar with the magnitude of the man's accomplishments.

This man also adored books. After all, he'd found her in a library. Moreover, he'd dedicated his life to science.

Men had so many options in their lives, and yet he'd chosen a life of the mind. A life of the *scientific* mind.

She tilted her head. "Would you like to accompany me to the coast?"

Her heartbeat quickened, but it was too late to take the words back now.

"Ah." He nodded solemnly. "You require an escort." He glanced at the clock. "I hadn't anticipated that question."

"Well, we've just met." Her cheeks warmed. "It was just a thought."

"A not entirely appropriate one." He scrutinized her.

"Perhaps not," she admitted, feeling her cheeks warm.

"But you do have a Scottish accent," he said in an understanding tone.

She waited for him to say something else, but he didn't.

"What does my accent have to do with it?" she asked finally.

"Ah, young lady. Everyone in England knows you Scots are all quite wild."

She drew back.

He gave a lackadaisical shrug. "But you can't help it. It's in your nature."

Her breath vanished.

"You mustn't worry about it," he said in an unctuous voice. "I can accompany you, if you would like."

"I-I think I'll go on my own," she squeaked.

He nodded gravely, clasping his eye monocle. "I look forward to seeing you again. You bring much amusement."

Well.

That was *almost* a compliment.

She nodded farewell rapidly and sped from the library, then hesitated.

Perhaps the man hadn't said precisely the correct thing, but wasn't everyone always saying *she* was saying the wrong thing? Had she unwittingly insulted people here when she'd first arrived in London?

She chewed on her bottom lip.

Perhaps.

She couldn't be certain she had not done so.

At any rate, he was a scientist and he was a far more appropriate match than anyone else at the castle. Unlike the Duke of Jevington, who had seemed cold when she'd last seen him, as if forcing himself to be unfriendly, even though unfriendliness was not a trait he commonly practiced, this man had made continuous eye contact.

Besides, Margaret tended to be proper herself. A man who was also proper, who was perhaps even *more* proper, could hardly be undesirable.

She rounded the corner, traversed the foyer and exited the castle, still musing on this fact.

CHAPTER ELEVEN

JASPER FOUND HIS FRIENDS and strode toward them. He pulled his hat down to shield himself from the sunbeams that danced about him. This was the best sort of day in England.

It was almost magical.

Brightling waved him over, and Jasper joined him.

"When are the other guests arriving?" Brightling asked.

"Oh, they've all arrived," Jasper said easily.

Brightling's eyebrows rose sharply.

"Do you find something surprising?" Jasper asked.

"I merely expected more guests," Brightling said.

"I've selected the very best ones," Jasper said.

Brightling nodded, no doubt conscious of the compliment. "You've never invited the Carberrys here before."

"Hence the urgency with which to schedule a gathering," Jasper said.

"Er—yes."

Brightling, despite his considerable capabilities in botany, had not developed an equal expertise in all subjects. Jasper was certain the man had not even hosted a party before. Miss Carberry's distaste for such events was no doubt something with which Brightling and she might exclaim over, in the peculiar mating ritual in which couples determined the most trivial similarities and exclaimed over them with an excitement best suited for other occasions.

In Jasper's opinion, a shared love for chocolate and croquembouches hardly sufficed in creating a happy marriage. Since Jasper did not suffer from shyness, he'd immersed himself in balls and house parties when not fulfilling his parliamentary and estate overseeing duties. He was accustomed to seeing hopeful expressions of debutantes transform to pride as they secured marriages, then transform to a less heartwarming sourness as they resigned themselves to unhappiness. Though everyone was eager to encourage people to marry, they were less prone to encourage appropriate diligence.

Brightling's lips veered into an uncharacteristic downward position.

"You're frowning," Jasper said.

"I had a thought," Brightling said.

"I can see why you're so reluctant to think, given your reaction," Ainsworth said, and the others chuckled.

Brightling pouted. "I merely thought Jasper might have invited Miss Carberry in the hopes of marrying her off to one of us."

Though Jasper believed in the virtues of veracity and had never considered himself a truth evader before, he hesitated to confirm Brightling's suspicions.

Ainsworth laughed. "That's the most absurd thing I've heard all day. And I spent the morning peer reviewing scientific articles." He shook his head, with the air of a man whose day had overflowed with ridiculousness, and yet had still not been sufficiently prepared for more.

"There's nothing to laugh about," Jasper said shortly.

"But Jasper..." Ainsworth protested. "Surely I needn't explain the inappropriateness of a match with her? And the hilarity of you, head rogue among rogues, to take on matchmaking duties with the zeal of a matchmaking mama... Why, it would be incredible. Utterly impossible."

"Any of you would be lucky to wed Miss Carberry." Jasper's face heated, and he rounded his hands into fists. "She is a woman of the utmost integrity."

Love was unlikely to come to these stalwart friends of his if they felt it planned. These men considered themselves leaders, as any man might do who regularly met with royals, and who commanded ducal estates. These men were wary of the prospect of manipulation. Despite their obvious respect for Jasper, a man was unlikely to leave his marital happiness to a man he'd first met clothed in a skeleton suit and carrying a hobbyhorse.

No, this was not the time for Jasper to confess everything. Even the most cursory supposition indicated that any confession would lead to mockery. Though Jasper would not mind being called Cupid, even if the word were accompanied by chuckles that would not serve to get anyone married.

And Miss Carberry needed to marry.

He'd promised her.

"Naturally I do not harbor any desires to be confused with an arrow-wielding baby," Jasper said stiffly. "Even if we do share similarly cherubic curls. I have no desire to marry off Miss Carberry."

"Of course." Ainsworth shot an irritated glance at Brightling. "It is obvious that was an absurd suggestion."

"A man might be fortunate to marry Miss Carberry," Jasper said staunchly, "but the process of marrying her off is a task for her parents."

Brightling gritted his teeth, and Jasper decided to halt his protestations. No need for the other dukes to mock Brightling. After all, Brightling's intuitive prowess had been correct.

Jasper cleared his throat. "I simply invited her because I found her intriguing. And I—er—wanted to learn about Mr. Carberry's business."

"You find trade intriguing?" Ainsworth asked.

"I find everything intriguing," Jasper said. "Now, who wants to play tennis?"

The others nodded, and Jasper beamed. None of his friends could best him in that sport. A man is bound to be wounded after being beaten while playing tennis, and in that state, a man is certain to take interest in a lovely, concerned female.

Jasper wouldn't need to tell Miss Carberry to be concerned: she would be, naturally. Miss Carberry had the air of a woman who wouldn't be disappointed in a man by his inability to strike a tennis ball with consistency.

Indeed, her presence could be described as soothing.

Jasper's heart soared, no doubt buoyed by renewed thought of his continued singledom. Obviously, his spirits were not lifted by the sheer thought of Miss Carberry. That would be ridiculous, and Jasper was not fond of the ridiculous.

When he'd spent a house party with her, he hadn't, in truth, paid much attention to her. But he'd certainly noticed she was no creator of negative attention. She did not mock others, and when her mother had tied her to his bed, she'd not sought to take advantage of the situation and trap him into marriage. On the contrary, she'd risked her life.

His friends could do much worse than Miss Carberry.

After he changed into his sport gear, he strode toward the tennis court. Birds chirped pleasingly, butterflies danced, and even slugs slid over the ground, attempting long journeys across the grass, undaunted by their limited exterior protection.

When he joined his friends, inhaling the scent of roses that wafted through the air, his thoughts did not drift far from contemplation of Miss Carberry. He remembered the brave manner in which she'd visited him so she could merely suggest they dance together, when the next season began. He remembered her kindness to her grandmother and dog. He also remembered something else, something he'd attempted to forget.

He remembered discovering her on his bed, and the manner in which her alabaster skin had glowed underneath the candlelight. He remembered the curve of her collar bone. He also remembered the manner in which her dress had been torn, revealing scandalously bare skin. And he remembered a deliciously curved body.

He craved to touch her, to trace the curve of her bosom, the curve of her hips with his fingers, with his lips.

His heart thudded, and he blinked into the sunlight, attempting to banish the sudden thought away.

A flash of dark hair shot in the distance before him, accompanied by a sliver of navy.

Miss Carberry had been wearing a navy dress. It had been the practical sort suited for travel that women embraced.

He scrunched his forehead.

No doubt he'd made a mistake. Miss Carberry was going to visit the library, not run about his estate. Miss Carberry seemed an unlikely candidate to be overtaken by athletic impulses. He'd had the impression she was more sensible.

After all, she was quiet.

Perhaps he'd simply conjured her in his mind. He wasn't in the habit of imagining people, and he would have suspected he'd be more likely to begin envisioning things in his mind by starting with something less complex: a lake, for instance.

Laughter sounded at some comment one of his friends had said.

He should be chatting with his friends, and not musing about Miss Margaret Carberry. After all, he was simply trying to find a husband for her: not fill his mind with thoughts of her. It was a simple task, one enjoyed by generations of matchmaking mamas, and one which Jasper intended to master.

And yet...

Miss Carberry *had* gazed toward the ocean. And she *had* seemed knowledgeable about this region. Was it possible she'd gone to the coast to hunt for fossils herself?

He frowned.

He hadn't thought she'd abandon the comforts of the library. If she wanted to explore the coast on her own, she could do so. This was hardly Seven Dials, and he trusted her not to get swept into the ocean.

Still, his stomach tightened as it always did when considering bodies of water. Jasper may have visited the continent on multiple occasions, but he never enjoyed the sea crossing. Imagining *other* people doing the crossing was worse.

"Coming?" Brightling tossed the ball in the air. "Time to play!"

Jasper stared at the ball.

Normally he didn't require any enticement to play.

And yet, even under this delightful sunshine, even with his dear friends, playing didn't seem sufficiently appealing. His mind lingered on Miss Carberry. What was she doing now? Was she wandering over the sand? Scurrying from cave to cave? Basking in sunbeams? Had she removed her shoes and was strolling through the water? He imagined her raising her dress, so her ankles were visible. He imagined water rushing over them, lapping against her body.

The air suddenly seemed devoid of moisture.

Perhaps, since she was new, the gentlemanly thing to do would simply be to show her around. Orient her.

She probably could find the ocean easily enough. The sound of the ocean waves crashing against the shore was the type of thing one was bound to notice. But she was still his guest, and perhaps he could point out other things.

He found himself nodding, and Brightling shot him a curious look.

"Are you quite fine?" Brightling furrowed his brow.

"Er—yes," Jasper said hoarsely. "All's well with me. I just realize I have something else to do."

Brightling raised his eyebrows.

"So, I'm just going to go," Jasper blurted, before Brightling asked more questions.

"But what about the game?"

"Play it yourselves," Jasper shouted, jogging toward the English Channel, unhampered by the uneven ground as he moved past his gardeners' neatly maintained paths.

CHAPTER TWELVE

MARGARET RUSHED TOWARD the coast. Her long locks toppled from their position, and she secured her cap with her one hand, lest it decide to flit into the channel, confusing the fish with its abundance of lace and ribbons. Dark strands flew across her face, controlled more by the wind than by Margaret's coiffure skills.

She avoided the dukes, sprinting hastily past them, not desiring to enter into another uncomfortable conversation with them. The leaves of the chestnut trees rustled in the wind, and birds chirped.

Were it another day, Margaret would have been content to search for birds and record the features of birds she did not recognize in her notebook.

But this wasn't a normal day, nor was it a normal weekend.

Today she was near the very coast where the most intriguing fossils in England had been discovered. The fossils resembled crocodiles. In fact, they didn't even look so dissimilar from huge birds. The fossils seemed to be of a completely new species, as if strange large creatures had once swam and strode along England's coast.

The chestnut trees disappeared. Long strands of grass covered the ground, accompanied only by the occasional daisy.

Margaret quickened her pace, wanting to immerse herself into this new world.

Finally, the English Channel appeared before her. Azure waves lapped against a tawny-colored beach. Fluffy clouds zigzagged the sky, as if to marvel at the area's beauty, rather than because of any plans to force water down upon it.

Birds chirped and sang, and wildflowers swayed in the breeze.

She was here.

Mary Anning had discovered large, intriguing fossils not far from here. What creatures had roamed this coast?

Margaret approached the cliff's edge. A path curved onto the beach, and she followed it, winding her way until she reached the shore. She settled onto the sand, listening to the waves. The sun shone brightly, casting everything into a golden light. She removed her gloves and touched the sand with her fingers. How lovely it would be to explore this coast thoroughly, to see if she could find anything similar to what Miss Anning had found.

There wasn't time for that now. She shouldn't even be here. Mr. Owens had made that fact clear, even if the area seemed lacking in typical dangerous qualities. No port was nearby, swarming with sailors eager to revel. Threats of Frenchmen invading had long ago diminished. There was no storm descending, forcing the tide to grow higher and to surge quickly over the shore. She wouldn't be dashing into one of the caves for shelter.

No.

Margaret could simply enjoy herself.

"Miss Carberry?" a male voice jolted her from her thoughts, and she jerked her head around.

She blinked toward bright light, masking the figure.

"I'm sorry to startle you," a baritone voice she recognized said.

Her heart flew: it was the duke.

She scrambled up, slipping on the sand, and he caught her in his arms.

"How are you?" he asked.

"Quite well, Your Grace." Her voice squeaked. At some point, her breath seemed to have left her. No doubt, it preferred lingering about him.

Now that she stood, the light no longer masked him. Rather, it illuminated his broad shoulders, chiseled face, and exquisitely tousled hair.

She touched her throat.

"I shouldn't have disturbed you," he said, and his cheeks seemed a tawnier color than before. "I wondered when you went off on your own."

"I'm quite happy on my own," she said.

"But you don't need to be."

"No," she admitted, and she found herself smiling. "I simply wanted to see the coast."

"Ah," he glanced toward the waves. "It is beautiful."

"Indeed."

"You are an admirer of beauty."

She hesitated. He expected her to agree.

"I am," she said, "but I'm also an admirer of fossils."

"Ah. But of course. Mary Anning, correct?"

"You heard of her discoveries?" For some reason she was surprised.

His lips twitched. "I am not solely concerned with festivities."

"Oh," she breathed.

"Though..." He looked down. "It is possible that I first heard about her at a party."

She giggled, and his eyes sparkled.

Fiddle-faddle.

She averted her gaze, lest he catch her staring.

It would be easy to linger her eyes on the manner in which the sunlight played in his hair, turning some of his tousled locks caramel.

The thought was hardly original to her. Other women remarked on the man's attractiveness, as they strove to determine which Greek God he most resembled.

"Discovering the bones of huge, ancient creatures," the duke continued. "Quite extraordinary."

"Indeed," she said, finding herself beaming.

"I've read that perhaps these fossils are remnants of large elephants that the Romans may have brought to Britain when they conquered the country."

Margaret frowned. "I have heard that theory."

"Yet you're not a proponent of it?"

"The fossils do not resemble elephants."

"They are large."

"That is not the only trait elephants possess. In fact, there's a similarity with birds I find fascinating."

He turned to her sharply. "So these creatures had feathers?"

She shook her head. "I wouldn't necessarily say that. But they may have at times strolled on two feet."

"So less similar to Lily."

"Precisely."

They strode along the coast, chatting about the implications of the discoveries. The sun continued to shimmer golden beams, the waves continued to sparkle with the force of diamonds, and the grass and wildflowers continued to sway elegantly under the wind.

"You must speak of your theories to Ainsworth," the duke remarked.

"Ainsworth?" Margaret's shoulders sank. For a blissful few moments, she'd managed to forget about the house party.

The duke nodded. "Ainsworth is most intellectual. He will find your ideas fascinating."

"You didn't give the impression of finding my ideas dull."

"N-Naturally not. But he will understand them more. He understands everything."

Margaret averted her gaze, lest the duke see her frown. She was certain the duke was much more intelligent than he seemed to think. Emma had told her that when he'd accompanied her future husband to the continent that the duke had been in possession of excellent language skills.

"Much like elephants are not the only large creatures, I suspect the Duke of Ainsworth is not the only intelligent duke."

He furrowed his brow. "You mean Brightling? He is quite the expert in flora and fauna."

"I meant you."

The duke's cheeks grew ruddy. "No one says that."

"Perhaps they should."

He looked at her curiously, and Margaret's heart trembled. She shouldn't go about complimenting him. Compliments might make him think that perhaps she held him in overly high regard. He'd arranged this entire event so he would not be saddled with her in the future.

"Perhaps I will speak with the Duke of Ainsworth," she acquiesced.

"Good, good," he said, but his voice seemed to lack its customary force, and Margaret wondered whether her feelings were already too clear.

She adopted a faster pace so they might reach the castle more quickly.

CHAPTER THIRTEEN

JASPER SHOULD HAVE been relieved to find his friends sitting in the drawing room when Miss Carberry and he returned to the castle, but instead an odd twinge of irritation moved through him. The feeling was not improved when Miss Carberry's mother and grandmother joined them. Lady Juliet was apparently not feeling well and would not join them, though Jasper suspected Lady Juliet was aware tonight was supposed to be about Miss Carberry.

Clearly, Lady Juliet was a good friend. Lady Metcalfe had also been close to Miss Carberry. Many people seemed to know Miss Carberry was wonderful. He only wished Miss Carberry would know it as well.

The conversation with Miss Carberry had ended, and he contented himself with his friends.

Finally, her father reappeared with their dog. Lily wagged her tail and rushed toward Margaret. Margaret exclaimed and petted Lily unselfconsciously, and something in Jasper's chest tightened at witnessing such obvious affection.

"Did you have a pleasant stroll?" Jasper asked.

"Oh, yes." Mr. Carberry beamed.

"The sun is setting," Mr. Carberry said. "I can see it from the window. It's beautiful."

Jasper widened his eyes. "You're jesting."

"Er—no." Mr. Carberry eyed him strangely. "It's not something I would jest about. *If* I jested."

Jasper threw his hands up in the air. Of course. It had been a foolish question. Mr. Carberry was not prone to jesting. He was unlikely to begin by attempting complex jokes about sun patterns. Most people new to the process favored placing a simple banana peel on strategic places on the ground—a hard surface was required for that particular effort at levity. Carpets would not do.

Jasper gazed at the window. The footmen would arrive with the first food soon, but Jasper resisted the urge to wallow away his regrets about sunsets while gobbling canapes. He needed everyone to be outside. *Now.* No matter how smug they might appear at their armchair selection.

"Let's go outside," Jasper said.

"Outside?" Ainsworth shot him a quizzical look.

"Naturally outside," Jasper snapped. "Outside isn't an absurd concept. After all, places are either inside or outside, and most places are the latter."

Brightling's mouth dropped open, but Miss Carberry's lips twitched.

Jasper headed toward the door, pivoting only to say, "this way."

"You want us to join you?" Ainsworth drew his forehead together.

"Naturally," Jasper said.

His friends shot one another odd glances, as if they found *him* peculiar.

He threw up his hands. "You needn't look so puzzled. The statement shouldn't be necessary. You did enter this way."

Miss Carberry lifted her eyebrows, and Jasper nodded.

She needed to come too.

This was important. Sunsets were one of nature's most consistently romantic occurrences. They seemed popular with everyone, even if he was grateful that men's fashion no longer demanded that one swathe oneself in pink as if to emulate one of the striking features of a sunset. Black suited him just fine: one worried far less about the occasional spillage and garden wanderings were not sources of stress.

Soon, they stepped onto the gravel. The castle soared behind them, casting a shadow, and Jasper shivered.

Unfortunately, shadows were not known for their romance inducing quality. Most people who spoke of shadows, when they mentioned them at all, categorized them with more fear-inducing things. If people lingered on the castle's shadow, they might contemplate the prospect of ghosts and whether they might reside in the castle.

Naturally, if ghosts did exist, they were bound to choose the castle as a residence. His guests simply didn't need to muse over that indisputable fact.

There were other things they could linger on: the scent of roses wafting from the nearby garden, the manner in which the light spilled over Miss Carberry's face, illuminating her soft skin. She gazed upward, dear thing, as if entranced in the sunset.

The others should be making conversation with her. They should be sharing the names of flowers and pondering the names' suitability for unborn children.

Miss Carberry strode beside her mother. Men tended to view mothers with suspicion, and in this case, any instinct to be wary of them was entirely well-founded. He could not blame his friends, who had not all seen one another recently, from taking the opportunity to chat with one another.

Jasper stared as Ainsworth began to speak with Miss Carberry. No doubt they were speaking of something intellectual. That was what Ainsworth tended to do, and Jasper had no doubt Miss Carberry was quite capable of following any conversation.

At Lord Metcalfe's house party, Miss Carberry had shared obscure subjects with ease. Jasper would consider himself proud to remember the names of any vertebrae, much less expound about a particular species' habits.

Barking sounded, and Jasper turned.

"Lily!" Mr. Carberry bellowed, despite his retiring nature.

Miss Carberry halted and glanced in the direction of the sound. Lily sped through the garden, wagging her tail.

"Lily!" Mr. Carberry bellowed again, with the force of a man auditioning to replace a bugle.

"Lily!" Mrs. Carberry and Miss Carberry said, their high-pitched voices joining in what would be in other circumstances a pleasant harmony.

He'd left the castle with too much haste. He hadn't even determined the door was closed, and the servants, doubtless, had been too bewildered to ascertain it.

He'd need to find Lily. He couldn't let something happen to her.

He took off at a run. His friends sprinted after him. Thuds sounded behind him, and a great many voices now shouted "Lily!"

It was of no avail.

Lily was content to run. She might halt when boredom set in, though regrettably, there was little in the estate to tire of. He feared the estate was filled with interesting scents and exciting small animals.

And this was Margaret's dog.

Margaret's dog that she'd raised from a puppy.

Margaret's dog that was one of the few connections with her previous life that she had.

And Lily might become lost, might become hurt, on his estate.

There was only one thing Jasper could do: follow the dog.

Jasper pounded over the estate, soon losing the others. Perhaps they were strong, but they didn't know every short cut here. Jasper did.

Unfortunately, Lily seemed to be heading for the water.

Blast it.

She'd spotted the ducks.

Jasper leaped over a gate that separated the rose garden from the orchards and sprinted toward her. He couldn't see anyone else now. It was up to him to not lose her. The sun was setting, and this was not a good time for a dog to be lost. If only this estate had hedges that enclosed it.

Lily leaped into the lake and paddled toward the island.

Jasper cursed.

She was in the water. That beastly, beastly water. The sort of water people drowned in. The sort of water his parents had drowned in. The sort of water his siblings had drowned in.

He stared at the liquid, imagining Lily being pulled below. Lily paddled, but her pace slowed in the water. Perhaps swimming was not one of her common pastimes.

He needed to get her.

Damnation.

He wasn't going to tell Margaret he'd let her dog drown.

Jasper leaped into the water. The water was wet and dreadful, but Jasper refused to turn back.

"Over here, Lily," Jasper said.

Lily tilted her head at him suspiciously. Still, she didn't move farther toward the island, and he swam toward her.

"Come," Jasper said again.

Then Lily swam toward him.

Jasper grinned.

Lily paddled rapidly, even passing him. Well, she was a good girl. She knew he wanted to be back on land.

Jasper turned to follow her, then halted.

Miss Carberry stood before him. The sunset glowed over her, casting rose and violet light over her.

She looked... beautiful.

"It's you," he said dumbly.

"I heard some splashes." She knelt and tied a ribbon she must have pulled from her dress onto Lily's collar.

"You're very practical," he said.

Her cheeks pinkened somewhat, and she focused on petting Lily.

Jasper looked about. "Where are the others?"

"They headed toward the coast."

"Oh. And you didn't follow?"

Her cheeks pinkened again. "I saw you going this way. I—er—hoped you had seen her."

"I thought you would prefer to stay with the dukes."

"I don't know how to speak with a duke," Miss Carberry stammered.

Jasper frowned. "You do realize I'm a duke."

"Well, yes. But that's different."

Jasper arched an eyebrow. "Are you saying I do not fulfill your ducal expectations? Am I not sufficiently imposing?"

"Not precisely," Miss Carberry admitted.

Jasper narrowed his eyes. He stepped toward her but was distracted by an odd squeaking sound. He frowned. "Did you hear that?"

Miss Carberry's lips twitched. "I believe you have water in your shoes, Your Grace."

Jasper contemplated those words and took another tentative step toward her. The same irritating noise sounded again, this time accompanied by distinct sloshing.

"This is why you don't think I'm respectable," he growled.

"I think you're perfectly respectable," Miss Carberry protested, her eyes sparkling. She shook her head, and for a moment he was distracted by her luscious midnight locks that had come undone from her pursuit. He resisted the temptation to run his fingers through her hair.

Jasper scrunched his brows, conscious water was dripping from his face in a distinctly unrespectable manner.

"I haven't forgotten you're a duke."

"I'm glad my soggy presence hasn't eliminated your memory, Miss Carberry," he said grumpily.

The woman grinned, and Jasper smiled back.

Few people were so genuine in their emotions. Most held them back when they found things amusing, and displayed them, when things were not amusing, as if they'd confused smiles with shields.

Lily wriggled her body.

"Oh, no," Miss Carberry said. "Lily, don't."

Lily increased her wriggles, and dirty water slammed into him. This time, Miss Carberry did laugh, and Lily barked joyfully.

Jasper should have frowned.

He should have scowled.

Blast it, he was certain even Miss Carberry would have been understanding if he'd *sworn*.

But instead he chuckled.

"Oh, you're a very bad girl," Miss Carberry said mournfully. "That's not polite. Most men don't like being covered in dirty water."

Lily wagged her tail, as if happy simply to be included in the conversation. Her adherence to morals was evidently of less importance.

"Come, let's go back to the manor house," Jasper said.

"Of course." Margaret handed him a shawl.

He eyed the red and pink cashmere, lined with gold fringes, with suspicion. "What's this?"

"It's to keep you warm."

"I can't use that," he said.

The shawl had flowers on it. Not that men went about wearing shawls that didn't have flowers. Shawls were an item of clothing not explored by men.

She rolled her eyes. "Please. Or do you want to get sick?"

Jasper pouted. "I never get sick."

"And you're willing to test that theory?"

He frowned and shifted his feet. Water sloshed from his attire, and his shirt remained drenched. As did his trousers. As did his tailcoat.

He was certain it hadn't been this chilly before he'd dove into the water.

"Or perhaps I should just give it to Lily," Miss Carberry said. "And then if you change your mind, you can take it from her."

Jasper's nostrils flared. "That won't be necessary."

Miss Carberry beamed and handed him the shawl. He sighed, then proceeded to dry himself off.

"You can let people help you," she said.

"I help others," Jasper said. "That more than suffices."

She looked at him curiously for a moment, and he wondered whether he'd said too much. Most likely he had. He felt off-kilter.

The sky had turned brilliant shades of pink and tangerine, but as they ambled, the sky darkened. Now that Jasper was no longer hopping over barriers, the path to the castle was longer.

A scent of vanilla emanated from her, and he inhaled.

Jasper had an odd temptation to kiss her. He wondered what it would feel like to draw her close to him. Her large eyes might widen, and her long thick eyelashes might flutter. Her cheeks might pinken.

Would her soft lips part? How might they feel against his own? How might...other parts of her body feel against his?

He swallowed hard, and she turned her head to him.

"Are you quite well, Your Grace?"

"I'm fine," he said, but his voice sounded oddly husky, and concern emanated from her large eyes.

Nobody looked at him with that concern.

His friends often teased him, seeming to find amusement in his quest for festivities. Even Lord Metcalfe, his closest friend from childhood and who had the estate adjoining his in Surrey, often hinted—strongly hinted, that Jasper should be serious.

Nobody worried about him.

Debutantes with oppressive mothers weren't supposed to look at him with concern.

The sensation wasn't entirely unpleasant. Miss Carberry emanated a calmness about her, despite all her troubles, and Jasper found himself relaxing in her presence.

The world had long since darkened, the sunset vanished during the search for Lily, but he found himself staring at the sky all the same. Stars sparkled ahead, glittering in such splendor he wondered why he did not stare at them every night.

"Thank you for finding, Lily," she said.

His heart squeezed, but he gave a nonchalant shrug. "I wanted to assist you."

"Your clothes are ruined."

"I have more clothes."

They strolled toward the castle. It loomed before them, its towers now merely a dark silhouette against the shimmering sky.

Somehow, it made the castle no less magnificent.

Lily wagged her tail as they proceeded back. It seemed impossible to imagine she'd been doing athletic feats before. She strode mellowly, calmed by the evening's adventure, and Jasper's heart felt full.

Was this what married life was like? Taking pleasant walks and discussing the day's events? It was unlike most time he spent with women.

Miss Carberry did not flutter her lashes with a speed matched only by the expert movements of her fan. She hadn't mentioned yet in the conversation that she was fully capable of managing a household and say that she could be depended upon to keep the servants in check. Miss Carberry hadn't spoken demeaningly of other women, women whom Jasper had considered her to be friends with, as if to not-so-subtly imply that she was the preferred choice.

Miss Carberry had absolutely no expectations of him.

The woman was most intriguing.

He glanced at her, even though it was dark. "You must find it odd to be so far away from Scotland."

"I do," she admitted, as if surprised the topic had evolved from the antics of dogs and attire maintenance to herself.

"Do you miss it very much?"

She hesitated. "Yes."

Somehow the answer made his throat dry, and an odd sensation, something very much like disappointment, thrummed through him.

"I'll always miss the landscape," Miss Carberry mused. "I hadn't expected to become so attached to the rugged slopes of hills. I hadn't thought I'd loved moss and rocks so much."

"Do you want to return?"

She sighed, then shook her head. "This is my life now. I have some friends in the capital. And my grandmother is here." She glanced at the dog. "And Lily."

Jasper nodded.

He understood.

"I've never been to Scotland," he admitted. "I think I would like it."

"You would."

He'd traveled often in his twenties, and last year he'd even gone to the German-speaking part of the continent with Lord Metcalfe, but he'd never ventured north. There was much he needed to learn. He couldn't simply do the Grand Tour every few years. There was more to the world than Italian sculptures crammed before canvases and tapestries.

There was nature itself.

Just as there were also quiet walks with a companion.

But then, Miss Carberry had been going on a quiet walk with a companion.

Ainsworth.

In truth, the Duke of Ainsworth, was extremely suited to Miss Carberry. Ainsworth had been top of his class in Eton, and top of his class at Cambridge. Even the tutors had seemed to indicate he did not need to excel to such an extent, given the fact his future was already set. Most men with large estates to manage did not write research articles.

But then, Ainsworth was not most men.

Jasper had struggled in school. He hadn't had a natural affinity for fractions and Latin declensions, and anything his tutors had managed to drum into him at the time had long since been forgotten. Truly, he wondered why he'd bothered to learn at all.

"So, there's no one who interests you?" he asked.

Miss Carberry was silent.

Suspiciously silent.

"Er—perhaps." She swept her hand through her hair and stopped to gaze at him. Her eyes hadn't seemed dull before, but now they gleamed with a definite confidence.

CHAPTER FOURTEEN

JASPER ALMOST DREW back.

He'd considered Miss Carberry to be given to formality, as so many of those studious were prone to do. The unfortunate truth was that knowing society rules and being sufficiently deferential in the presence of one's elders was unlikely to suffice in endearing one to the *ton,* even if following rules strictly was the sort of thing that would get one top mark's from one's tutor. He doubted governesses' grading systems varied widely.

Miss Carberry's cheeks had pinkened becomingly, and Jasper found himself beaming back.

He *did* have good friends.

"Now tell me, which duke caught your eye? Was it Ainsworth? Or Hammett? It so often is Hammett. That man is quite the boxer. Sonnets have been written on his upper body strength."

Miss Carberry widened her gaze for a moment, then shook her head. "Oh, no."

"You find them lacking?"

"They're fine," she said hastily. "But not appropriate for me."

"They're not good enough for you?" Jasper pondered this. Miss Carberry was very good.

"I am certain they are quite good," she amended. "Truly."

"Yet you have reservations?"

She nodded miserably. "I know it's important for you that I find a husband."

He furrowed his brow. It had been important, but it had been because he'd desired to help her.

"So, you should be relieved to learn that I have found a potential prospect."

"Oh."

Jasper scrutinized her. Surely most women wouldn't have such glazed expressions when contemplating spending the rest of one's life with someone who wasn't a duke. Besides, Jasper knew the guest list. He'd chosen an intimate house party. Large house parties might have considerable advantages, but he'd suspected Miss Carberry's quiet nature might be overwhelmed by the incessant laughter and passionate discussions that his house parties seemed to so inevitably inspire.

Good Lord. Had she fallen for someone inappropriate? The point of having her find a husband was for her to marry someone lofty, someone who would make her happy. And of course, the last thing Jasper required was for Mrs. Carberry to be upset at him. The woman acted sufficiently unpredictable without having reason to be angry at him. He was certain if Miss Carberry decided to run off with one of Jasper's staff, Mrs. Carberry would feel entitled to expressing that emotion.

"My footmen do tend to have regular features," Jasper said.

"Your footmen?" Miss Carberry jerked her head toward him.

"And my gardeners," Jasper acknowledged. In truth, his gardeners did possess that healthy gleam people liked. Their attire might be less formal, but no doubt that had advantages.

He only hoped none of the gardeners had practiced this with Miss Carberry.

"I am not referring to one of your staff," Miss Carberry said sternly. "That would be—" She shook her head. "Well, it wouldn't be *right*."

"Then who exactly are you referring to?"

"Mr. Octavius Owens, of course," Miss Carberry said.

Jasper furrowed his brow.

Miss Carberry sighed. "He works with your friend, the Duke of Ainsworth."

"Oh." Jasper blinked. "I suppose I need to make his acquaintanceship."

"You'll see more of him," Miss Carberry said confidently. "He enjoys a close friendship with the duke."

"Ah." Jasper frowned.

Perhaps his thoughts truly had been elsewhere when his friends had arrived. He'd been distracted thinking of his plans for the house party, and he must have neglected to hear Hammett talk about his friend.

"And how did you speak with him?" he queried.

For some reason the question seemed to make Miss Carberry's delectable cheeks pinken.

"It's—er—not important."

He raised an eyebrow, and she inhaled.

"There may have been an—er—tripping incident in the library."

"He tripped? How clumsy."

"Er—" Her cheeks pinkened. "Mr. Owens did not trip."

Guilt swerved through Jasper, and he cursed himself.

"Not that it's bad to trip," he said awkwardly.

"It *is* clumsy," she admitted.

"I hope you're not hurt."

"I'm entirely fine," she reassured him hastily. "And it was entirely my fault."

There was that customary niceness again.

"I assume this Mr. Owens was not responsible for your incident?" Jasper asked.

"N-No," Miss Carberry said. "But he witnessed it. And then he came and helped me up."

Well.

It was scarcely knight in shining armor material, but Jasper supposed that not everyone could act with his remarkable gallantry.

If Miss Carberry had fallen, he would have rushed toward her. He would have pulled her into his arms so she would not need to rise inelegantly from the floor, and he would have carried her to the nearest chaise-longue. He envisioned the scene happily, until he remembered Miss Carberry had fallen earlier this month, and no one had been there to assist her.

Miss Carberry deserved better.

"What did you talk about with him?" Jasper asked.

She shrugged. "Books."

Well. That shouldn't be a surprise. Most people might discuss books in libraries. It was the sort of topic that would occur one to speak about with higher frequency.

"He suggested another book for me to read," he continued. "He noticed I was carrying a copy of Gulliver's Travels. He was concerned the subject matter might be...unsuitable."

"He warned you about reading?" Jasper's brows soared upward, with the speed of bullets.

"Well, it was Jonathan Swift," Miss Carberry explained.

Jasper inhaled. "How horrendous."

"You enjoy Jonathan Swift?" Surprise sounded in Miss Carberry's voice, and he wanted to tell her that he did. He wanted to tell her he had multiple intellectual passions that equaled hers.

Unfortunately, that would not be true.

"In truth, I rather avoid reading in general," Jasper admitted. "But that doesn't mean some person should go about warning people against reading. Anyone should read what they desire to read."

"Oh." Miss Carberry stared at him. "That's an unusual sentiment."

He shrugged. He had a similar generous philosophy on merrymaking, and though Jasper did not understand why someone would want to sit still for hours while holding up some leather-bound pages, he did know it made some people happy.

Miss Carberry, no doubt, belonged to that category of people who took pleasure in such an odd activity.

Well, let her read.

This Mr. Owens should not be discouraging her from it.

"You should read the book," Jasper said firmly.

"I will," Miss Carberry said. "Despite the man's recommendations on books on botany."

Jasper shuddered. "That sounds even more tiresome than a novel."

Miss Carberry exhaled. "I'm afraid I've given you the wrong impression on the man. He's really quite nice."

"Be careful."

"But you wanted me to marry."

Jasper's eyes widened. He'd never even met this man. Why was Miss Carberry speaking of marrying him? He was vaguely aware this was probably his fault, though he did not like to linger on the subject. Perhaps he shouldn't have so enthusiastically declared this was her weekend to find a husband. It was the sort of statement bound to put romantic notions in a person's head. But then, he'd hardly thought to vet his friends' guests. Miss Carberry was supposed to choose a husband from one of his friends.

"He was simply making conversation," Miss Carberry said, her voice trembling.

Jasper sighed. "I hope so."

Women could be far too nice, and he thought Miss Carberry might succumb to that quality. After all, she exuded pleasantness. She'd been so nice she'd sneaked from his room when she'd had the chance to claim him for a husband, and she'd been so nice she'd evidently forgiven her mother's actions.

"Perhaps you needn't always be nice," he said.

She raised her eyebrows. "You don't want me to be nice?"

"I want you to be happy."

"Your Grace!" A voice shouted, and Jasper groaned.

"Your Grace!" A different loud, bellowing cry sounded. It was unmistakable to hear the slight tinge of accent.

He'd forgotten about his new hires.

He'd been enjoying his stroll with Miss Carberry and he braced himself for the moment to end.

Murmurings sounded, then Lily began to bark.

Blast.

"Who is that?" Miss Carberry asked.

"Those would be my bodyguards," Jasper said.

"They are most intimidating."

Jasper nodded proudly. He'd made good hires.

She giggled. "You needed two bodyguards to protect yourself from my mother?"

"It's not so absurd," he said. "Besides, who knows which other of my servants she might be bribing. Those trunks were quite large. It could be filled with a great deal of coin."

She laughed again, and his heart sang.

Unfortunately, the sound also acted as a beacon for more things than joy, for in the next moment, the two guards rushed toward them, their pace unhampered even by the darkness.

"Your Grace!" One of the men shouted, and his bald head glinted in the moonlight. He turned to his companion. "He's with that woman!"

His new hires sprinted toward Jasper and Miss Carberry, then pulled Jasper away.

Clearly, their athleticism was not confined to strength. These men excelled at speed as well.

Lily began to bark, but even though any man in possession of any sense may have been wary of approaching her, these men experienced no such qualms. Evidently, they were either sufficiently well-trained or sufficiently conscious of Jasper's generous paychecks, that they did not let a dog frighten them.

"We're here for you now," one of the men said in a soothing tone a doctor may have envied.

"Good," Jasper said. "But it's truly not necessary—"

In the next moment, Jasper's words were swallowed. Strong arms swept around his waist, and he was turned upside down and placed over the man's shoulders.

This would not do.

Nobody put Jasper over his shoulder.

He cleared his throat. "Put me down!"

The man did not put him down. "Don't worry, Your Grace!"

Jasper gritted his teeth. "This is embarrassing and unnecessary."

"We're just protecting you," the man said reassuringly.

Lily lunged at the man, and in the next moment the man took off, displaying the same speed as he and his companion had shown before.

The world bobbed curiously. In vain, he attempted to loosen himself from his bodyguard's grasp.

Lily continued to bark, and Miss Carberry reassured her.

Jasper groaned.

Hiring bodyguards had seemed like an excellent idea.

Perhaps he'd acted too hastily, just as everyone said he did, and he'd only succeeded in being ridiculous.

"Jasper?" Ainsworth's startled voice drifted toward him.

Evidently, not everyone had returned to the house yet.

He pointed in the direction of Miss Carberry, but when Ainsworth turned, Jasper wondered why he didn't feel as relieved as he should.

CHAPTER FIFTEEN

MARGARET STARED AS the two men hauled Jasper away.

Lily whimpered, no doubt wondering at the speed at which their new friend had abandoned them.

Men normally weren't carried off in that manner. Perhaps dukes were every bit as eccentric as they were rumored to be.

The sound of footsteps padding hastily away diminished, and Margaret suddenly felt very alone.

The roses still wafted a pleasant scent, mingling with that of the chestnut trees. The moon still shone above, still accompanied by shimmering stars, larger and more magnificent than the most expensive diamond necklace. Even the castle's silhouette in the distance remained present, imbuing everything with enchantment.

But the Duke of Jevington was no longer with her. She knelt down and petted Lily, murmuring words of comfort.

No doubt he hadn't intended to leave in such a dramatic fashion. Surprise had sounded in his voice.

At least, she thought she remembered surprise in his voice. Now, she was uncertain just what had occurred. Even if he had been surprised, it was clear his two employees had thought they were acting in his interests. Saving him *had* been mentioned.

Her heart tightened.

She didn't want to be the sort of woman a man needed saving from.

She resisted the urge to linger in the garden. Even the thought of marching back to where they'd found Lily had a definite appeal. She didn't want to reenter the castle. Not now. Not, in truth, ever.

"Miss Carberry?" A voice interrupted Margaret's musing, and she drew back.

She soon recognized the Duke of Ainsworth.

"Good evening," she said.

Her voice wobbled slightly, unaccustomed to making conversation with men. The fact he was a duke and no doubt known to all society did not improve matters.

"I see Jevington left in a hurry."

"Yes," she said simply.

"And you found your dog. Your father will be happy."

"Good," Margaret said briskly. She contemplated the man, wondering why people termed conversation so pleasant. After all, the man had not told her anything she'd not already known. Yes, the duke had left hastily, and yes, her father would be happy to be reunited with Lily.

"I'm sorry," the man said. "I only meant to congratulate you."

"Oh." She stiffened. "I see. Well—thank you."

"I'm afraid I must apologize on Jevington's behalf," the Duke of Ainsworth said.

"Oh." She tilted her head. "Do you do that often?"

"Nonsense." He chuckled, and her mood lightened.

"That would take far too long," the Duke of Ainsworth said, and her newfound exuberance halted abruptly.

Oh.

"But he's not a horrible fellow," the Duke of Ainsworth added.

"I suppose there are worse ways to describe someone," she admitted.

"I mean, he's a decent chap."

"How do you know him?" Margaret asked.

"Besides our status? At every dinner party, we're placed near one another. People enter a room ranked from highest ranked to less highly ranked, and our titles tend to put us together."

Margaret was silent. She lacked any title. She didn't even have a relation, however distant, who had a title. Her father had simply been one of the many Carberrys in his region, and then he'd rapidly become more. Much more.

"We also attended the same school," the Duke of Ainsworth said. "Eton."

"Then you must know him well."

"Yes."

Margaret wanted to ask him more questions. Learning more about the Duke of Jevington seemed a valuable occupation of her mind.

But it wouldn't be proper to do that, so she remained silent.

They strode toward the castle entrance.

"How are you familiar with him?" the Duke of Ainsworth asked suddenly.

"Me?" Margaret's voice squeaked.

She hardly wanted to tell him the truth. "I went to a recent ball of his."

She refrained from telling him she'd been in the duke's chambers, and that she was intimately aware with the duke's bed. Such things would be entirely improper to linger on. He could simply imagine they'd met downstairs, perhaps on the dancefloor, or perhaps near the punch table.

"And we were at a mutual house party," she added. "Not that we spoke then."

She sensed the Duke of Ainsworth was scrutinizing her, and she regretted she'd termed things thus. It wasn't very natural that they'd been at the same house party and barely talked. Most people were far better at talking.

"He must think very highly of you to invite you here," the Duke of Ainsworth said. "He enjoys his privacy."

"But he's always throwing balls. And dinner parties."

Clearly, the Duke of Jevington's friend had got it wrong.

"He likes doing things for other people," the Duke of Ainsworth said. "There's a difference."

"Oh." She blinked.

The Duke of Jevington was very helpful. Even at Lord Metcalfe's house party, he'd been helpful to his friend.

"You know he had some younger sibling?"

She jerked her head toward him. "No."

"He did."

Margaret didn't fail to note the man's use of the past tense. People didn't just happen to refer to a person's siblings in the past tense.

"So, they're dead?" her voice wobbled.

"They died in a carriage accident with his parents. They were fetching him at Eton. And then they hit a rock, and their carriage fell into a river, and they were no more."

"That's horrible," she breathed.

"Yes. He was the first one of us to lose his father. But he lost both his parents. He lost his whole family. That's why I think he likes being helpful. He knows what it is to suffer, and he doesn't want anyone to do that. Even if he fills his home with festivities, it's all for other people. Most families never picked up their sons from Eton. Jasper's family was particularly close, and he's conscious he wouldn't have any of this, if they hadn't perished thus."

"How dreadful," she murmured.

"Quite. He's still very wary of water."

"He swam in the lake to fetch Lily."

The Duke of Ainsworth turned his head to her sharply. "Most interesting."

Her heart ached at the tragedy she'd been unaware of. When she'd first met the Duke of Jevington, she'd dismissed him as a reveler, even if he did decidedly belong to the attractive type. She'd been wary of his generosity, but now everything made sense.

They came to the door of the castle, and the Duke of Ainsworth offered her his arm. "Let's find the others."

CHAPTER SIXTEEN

AFTER HIS VALET HELPED him make a hasty switch to evening attire of the non-dripping, non-soggy variety, Jasper retired to the drawing room inside his castle.

The other dukes and Mr. and Mrs. Carberry were there. Evidently, his servants had taken the initiative to round them up.

He didn't see anyone who met the description of Mr. Owens. He knew these people. He remembered that Miss Carberry had met Mr. Owens in the library.

He rose rapidly. "I—er—should leave."

Brightling scrunched his forehead together. "You just arrived."

"One of my buttons feels loose," he squeaked and hurried away.

It was unnerving to look for guests he didn't know in his own home. Jasper strode hastily over the corridor, lest he miss the arrival of Ainsworth and Miss Carberry. Obviously, it simply wouldn't be gentlemanly to not be present when Miss Carberry arrived. Certainly, there was no other reason he was eager to not tarry.

Fortunately, in the library he soon found a dark-haired man with a pale face. No doubt this was the lauded Mr. Octavius Owens.

Jasper scrutinized Mr. Octavius Owens, this apparent paragon among men. Jasper had expected the man to resemble an Adonis, and for a moment he thought he might have confused this man with the correct Mr. Owens. The man's hair didn't curl in an angelic manner, and he didn't look like he'd been snatched from a painting, as if even the Lord, upon looking at it, had to make certain this person existed. His height could only have been described as normal, and his shoulders did not lend themselves to comparisons with world-carrying beings made famous in Greek myths.

Indeed, normal was the chief word Jasper would have ascribed to him. Lesser men may have termed him mediocre. Though the man's figure was not overly rotund or thin, his appearance was unremarkable.

Yet Jasper should have known Miss Carberry was too sensible to choose a potential mate merely by his ability to increase one's heartbeats each minute. Miss Carberry wouldn't select a man by his ability to copy whatever musical rhythm might be emanating around him, and she would be too sensible to choose a man simply for his ability to tell romantic stories of him slashing enemies while attired in the Crown's uniform.

Jasper approached him.

Somehow Mr. Owens appearance still unsettled him. Because this wasn't the appearance of a man selected more for his fulfillment of childhood fantasies and ideals. If Margaret wanted to be with this man, it must be because she loved him. Except Margaret had only met him once... An odd, unpleasant feeling surged through Jasper.

"Your Grace." Mr. Owens flung himself into a deep bow, removing his top hat before it bounced onto the floor. He clutched onto it with the triumph of a man unaccustomed to feats of athleticism, then rose. "It is a pleasure to meet you."

"Very good to meet you," Jasper said.

After all, Miss Carberry would be happy, and Miss Carberry's happiness was important.

"Ah! I must say the same to you." The man darted into another obsequious bow, extended an arm up in perfect perpendicularity to the floor. When Mr. Owens raised his torso, his cheeks remained a distinct rosier color than previously.

Well. Politeness was an excellent quality in a husband. Jasper tapped his fingers together. Perhaps most debutantes did not muse about the importance of finding polite men, but that was surely an oversight. Trust Miss Carberry to know this.

"It is a great honor to be here with you," Mr. Owens continued eagerly. "I have been most looking forward to this occasion."

"How nice."

Jasper had been foolish to doubt that Mr. Owens was suitable for Miss Carberry. No doubt her presence was responsible for the buoyancy of Mr. Owens' personality.

"There will be some other people you know," Jasper said.

Mr. Owens raised an eyebrow.

"Mr. and Mrs. Carberry," Jasper said.

"Ah. Of Scotland." For a moment a flicker of irritation seemed to desire to reside on his face, but the moment soon passed.

"Their daughter is also attending," Jasper said gently, waiting for the man's reaction.

This was a house party. Mr. Owens would know that he would have a closer proximity to Miss Carberry than he could ever hope to have in London. Not for him would be the strictly two dance policy of the capital. Not for him would be visits that would not be extended longer than one might take to finish a pot of tea.

Mr. Owens would be able to pop into Miss Carberry when they both admired a particularly pretty rosebush, and they would be able to discuss whatever it was intelligent people discussed for hours over the breakfast table as footmen made certain their coffee cups were full.

Jasper would have Mr. Owens proposing in no time, and he would never worry again that Mrs. Carberry might persist with her marriage efforts. Happiness was soon advancing, even if he couldn't actually feel the emotion yet. No doubt Jasper simply needed to make certain that the door was open for it to enter.

"I know Mr. Carberry and his family only slightly," Mr. Owens said.

Jasper acknowledged the statement with an inclination of his head. "Even a short time can be sufficient in knowing them."

"Er—yes." Mr. Owens frowned, then stared at Jasper, as if hoping he might give some indication on his thoughts of the Carberry family so Mr. Owens might know how to best proceed.

Evidently the man was not going to venture into a soliloquy on the marvels of Miss Carberry. Jasper supposed he might be intimidating. Perhaps Mr. Owens reserved his romantic outbursts for visits to public houses with his friends, where he might later blame any effusiveness and sentimentality on the strength of his ale.

Miss Carberry was quiet, and she'd chosen a man who equaled her in that regard. Jasper only hoped Mr. Owens also equaled Miss Carberry in intelligence and kindness.

Jasper was happy.

Obviously.

Naturally he wasn't vexed he'd been hauled from his conversation with Miss Carberry. The point of having her come here wasn't for them to converse together. That would be absurd.

He had his friends to converse with. He didn't need to occupy Miss Carberry's time as she sought to find a suitable husband.

Naturally, that was good news.

Jasper strode back toward the drawing room. He peeked out a window, wondering if Margaret was outside. He hoped she hadn't become lost.

Margaret was outside, accompanied by Ainsworth.

Jasper frowned, and his fists tightened. No doubt they would both make excellent conversation, since they were both bright and clever. Most likely the moonlight continued to cast alluring beams over Margaret, casting her in a golden glow that should make any man in possession of eyes to have his heart squeeze.

This is what I wanted.

They were well matched.

Better than the odious Mr. Owens, no matter what Margaret might think about suitability.

Jasper entered the drawing room.

"You're looking sullen there," Brightling said casually.

"Nonsense." Jasper cast a glance at Mr. and Mrs. Carberry.

After all, Jasper made a point of not being sullen. Life was too short to be sullen. He'd decided that long ago. He gestured to the violinists. For some reason, he hadn't truly wanted them to play. The castle seemed sufficiently romantic. But he reminded himself that this was a time for romance.

After speaking with Miss Carberry at length, he was more convinced that she deserved everything in the world, and most people in the world agreed that Ainsworth was the epitome of the very best sort of man.

The musicians began to play their melodic tone, and his heart jerked.

He'd worked hard to select romantic pieces for the musicians to play. Obviously, he'd succeeded magnificently. After all, his heart normally didn't jolt and lurch in odd manners. It was clearly influenced by music.

There was one more step in preparing the castle, and he sighed. If he was going to ensure Miss Carberry's and Ainsworth's everlasting happiness, he couldn't do anything half-way. He glanced at a vase of roses on the mantle. There was everything lovely about the vase, but it was hardly completely necessary. The room was filled with vases brimming with roses.

He removed the roses from the vase, ignoring the manner in which the thorns pierced his skin. Then he pulled petals off.

"What are you doing?" Brightling asked.

"I just think these petals will look nice on the floor," Jasper said.

Brightling's eyes bulged.

"Not over the whole floor," Jasper assured her.

"*That* would be odd," Brightling said, still eying him strangely.

Jasper nodded absentmindedly and focused on pulling off the petals from the stems. He then went to the entrance, striding past the butler, then proceeded to scatter the petals from the main door toward the reception rooms.

"Your Grace?" Powell's eyes bulged in the same curious manner as Brightling's eyes had.

"Just decorating," Jasper said breezily.

"Are these to be an—er—permanent decoration, Your Grace?" Powell asked.

"Just for the duration of the house party," Jasper said. "You better have the housekeeper tell the maids to put fresh petals there each morning."

The butler inhaled, seeming to draw more air than was his normal habit. "Very well, Your Grace."

MARGARET ENTERED THE castle with the Duke of Ainsworth.

"Welcome," the butler said. "May I congratulate you on your success on finding your dog?"

"It was all the duke," Margaret said.

"The Duke of Jevington," the Duke of Ainsworth said, and the butler nodded his comprehension.

Lily wagged her tail as she entered. The butler closed the door hastily, and Margaret removed Lily's makeshift lead.

Petals were strewn over the floor, and the Duke of Ainsworth raised his brows. "I would have noticed these before."

"Indeed, Your Grace." The butler nodded. "I have no doubt you would have been able to do so."

Lily investigated the petals, sniffing some with her snout, and crushing others as she padded over them toward the reception hall.

The butler helped Margaret with her pelisse, and the Duke of Ainsworth handed some outdoor items to the butler as well.

Violin music drifted into the room, and despite herself, Margaret let out a sigh. She took the Duke of Ainsworth's proffered arm, and they proceeded into the reception room. The others stood rapidly as they entered. Surprise shown on Mama's face, but then she shot Margaret a pleased smile.

Margaret dropped her hold on the duke's arm. She hardly wanted her mother to get romantic notions about Margaret with him or any of these other men. Mama had brought a great many items with her, and it was entirely possible that one of the items might be rope.

"You're back." The Duke of Jevington bowed, but his demeanor seemed more guarded somehow.

Lily showed less restraint. She bounded into the Duke of Jevington's arms with enthusiasm, then rushed to Papa showing him similar affection.

"We can put Lily in our room," Mama said.

"Nonsense," the Duke of Jevington said.

Lily rushed back to him, and he bent to pet her.

"Shall we go eat? The servants have worked hard to keep the food warm, but I would not like to test the powers of the natural world more."

Margaret nodded. The duke's tone possessed an additional formal veneer that it had lacked earlier. Perhaps the man was simply hungry. He had worked heroically to find Lily. People tended to act oddly when they were hungry.

She followed the others into the dining hall. Everyone was happy when the footmen began to place enticing dishes before them. The dining room was beautiful: red silk lined the walls, giving the room a cozy quality despite the high ceilings, elaborate wood paneling and large hearth. Still, it was impossible for the dining room to compete with the food splayed over the long table. Everything appeared delicious.

Margaret knew. She knew every dish.

She turned. "It's Scottish."

He shrugged nonchalantly. "Indeed."

"B-But." She stared. She'd been to festivities before. She'd even attended dinner parties given to honor her father. But she'd hadn't been served Scottish food at a single of those events. "I don't understand."

He smiled, and his gaze was once again warm. "Don't tell me you're not familiar with these dishes. They were created by Chef Parfait. I'm afraid none of our kitchen staff are actually Scottish. They're probably all up there, enjoying their easy access to black pudding."

Her heart felt oddly light, as if it bobbed against her throat, but she still managed to thank him, even if her voice *did* squeak.

He'd spoken to her about Scotland today, but he wouldn't have had time to have people prepare such foods. This must have been planned in advance.

Her heart glowed, and perhaps something shown in her face, for he stiffened and cleared his throat. "Everyone, please note that Miss Carberry comes from Scotland. It is a beautiful land with a good cuisine."

Her parents stared at him oddly, and he shifted in his chair. He turned to the dukes. "Do you not like Scotland?"

"Oh, yes."

"Yes, indeed."

"Absolutely."

All the other dukes nodded and murmured their assent. The violinists entered the room. They shifted to a Scottish reel, and even though Margaret was not overly fond of dancing, she thought she could have easily made an exception.

After all, her heart was already dancing. It twirled and pirouetted merrily, undaunted by its lack of feet. Candlelight glowed throughout the room, gleaming from golden candelabras. From time to time she glanced at the Duke of Jevington. He sat at the head of the table, but he did not use the opportunity to utter into monologues relating to his greatness, his family's greatness, and his plans for his future's inevitable continued greatness. Instead, he managed the conversation, as if to make certain everyone felt included, and that everyone was able to voice an opinion in the conversation.

Though the dukes had seemed bewildered when she'd first met them, she soon learned they were all different, and not simply in how their consistently pleasant appearance was manifested in various standards of beauty.

Mr. Owens eagerly explained the importance of every bill and his own indisputably important role in the writing of each part of it. Commas were essential in legal matters, and Mr. Owens had been tasked with checking all of them. Margaret had hoped she might sit beside him, but the man pontificated so freely, she still learned more about him. At least, she learned of Mr. Owens' utter delight of having been included and the similarly important people he'd met over his lifetime. The Duke of Ainsworth of course was very intellectual and was an expert in the classics, and she chatted with him.

Most people forgot their Latin after school, but Margaret had a particular fondness for reading the exciting stories in the Aeneid. Somehow, it was comforting to know that the *ton* had not existed forever, and that once everyone had followed different rules entirely, rules that had become forgotten.

After dinner, the violinists followed them to the drawing room. The Duke of Brightling whispered something to them, then sat at the piano. Soon, they played a quadrille. Uncharacteristically, Papa led Mama to the center of the room. The Duke of Ainsworth quickly took Margaret's hand and led her beside them. The Duke of Jevington gave a stiff smile, then led Margaret's grandmother to the dance floor.

Margaret didn't want to dance.

She didn't like dancing.

But perhaps because Lily was found, perhaps because the Duke of Jevington had created such a pleasant environment, or perhaps because she simply didn't want to refuse the Duke of Ainsworth, she began to dance.

And it wasn't utterly horrible.

Sometimes the Duke of Jevington's gaze fell on her, and she shivered.

If only their stroll hadn't been curtailed. There were more things to chat about with him, though they could hardly speak while bobbing about.

She wasn't counting the days until the trip would end, as she normally did when she left the house.

CHAPTER SEVENTEEN

JASPER WAS THE BEST matchmaker in the world.

Both Ainsworth and that Owens fellow seemed taken with Miss Carberry, and if she only spent more time with the others, he was certain she would charm them too. It didn't matter in the least that Miss Carberry didn't seem to know all the steps, or at least, had added an additional one comprised of trampling on her dance partner's feet at odd moments.

Everything was proceeding perfectly.

His bodyguards sat in a corner of the room, slouched against the wall, their arms wrapped around themselves, as if to disguise the size of their fists from a possible attacker.

Perhaps hiring them *had* been excessive.

After all, the worst thing that might happen to Jasper was that he might marry Miss Carberry. And that was hardly a terror-inducing thought, even if he'd always imagined that marriage would be postponed. No, whichever man married her would be fortunate. He would have an intelligent partner in his life.

Jasper took another sip of his champagne. The bubbles leaped from the flute, as if desiring to take part in the dancing.

The song ended, and Miss Carberry yawned. "I think I shall retire now."

"You want to leave?" His voice sounded higher than he'd desired, and she raised her eyebrows.

"It's bedtime."

In three days, Miss Carberry and all his other guests would return to London, as if this house party had never occurred.

He'd assumed this house party would be tedious, as was so often the case when people from differing backgrounds were thrown together, like a cook, flummoxed by his choice of spices, who'd decided to not put anything in at all. He'd been prepared for courteous conversation that verged on the stilted: polite inquiries about the beauty of Scotland followed by vague professions of interest to one day visit there, when everyone knew the roads to Scotland were appalling and one was far more likely to visit the continent.

And yet somehow, that had not occurred.

"We haven't danced yet," Jasper said.

Miss Carberry widened her eyes. "You want to dance with me?"

Jasper nodded. He despised the slight insecurity in her voice.

Of course, he wanted to dance with her.

He gestured to the musicians. "Keep on playing."

They nodded, then started a languidly paced waltz. He refrained from frowning, though the temptation was palpable.

This was the sort of romantic music the musicians could have been playing when she'd danced with Brightling or Hammett.

Because obviously it was the music that sent odd tremors rushing through him when he took Miss Carberry's hand. That was the only explanation for it.

He'd thought her quite unremarkable when he first saw her, but then, she hadn't been following the careful scripts of other women. She'd been quiet, with large eyes that observed him, as if she knew everything about him. As if she merely had to look, and she...knew.

A faint vanilla scent wafted toward him. He inhaled the warm fragrance, reminding him of delicacies and deliciousness.

She swept her long lashes upwards, and a shy smile settled onto her face.

Heavens.

The woman emanated innocence. He felt dreadful for bringing all these men here for her. He'd had it all wrong. Other debutantes might have been cool and calculating in her position. They might have interrogated each man subtly, in between ample references to their own brilliance.

Miss Carberry hadn't stated her skills with fossils, her interest in birds, her love of animals, and her vast knowledge of literature.

He spun around with her, conscious of her hands on his shoulders, as his hands rested on hers. He stared into her eyes, and for a strange moment it occurred to him that it might be quite pleasant to kiss her. The world spun about them, and furniture and people blurred together.

But he couldn't fail to see her. He couldn't fail to see the softness of her pinkening cheeks, the manner in which her dark eyes glimmered, and the swoop of her upturned nose. How had he never realized that her heavy dark brows bestowed her a regal quality? Her olive-green dress was an unusual choice. Most women seemed to favor colors found on petals: whites and pinks, blues and purples. They never chose olive. And yet... The color emanated its own sophistication.

Suddenly Jasper felt ill at ease. Miss Carberry lived in a world he knew little about, a world filled with all manner of facts. He'd sat her beside Ainsworth, and he could swear he'd heard them discuss Latin words. Even finishing fighting the French had not brought him as much joy as had closing his Latin book forever.

The dance ended, and he continued to stare, wishing they might dance more, feeling there was more he wanted to learn. Unlike other gaps in his knowledge, it felt vital he rectify his lack of expertise.

She stepped away, and he nodded to the musicians that they might halt their playing.

Somehow, he didn't want to see her dance with anyone else anyway. He'd spent much time orchestrating this event, but it failed to usher in the anticipated joy. Miss Carberry would marry someone: it seemed absurd that he'd worried. Perhaps when he'd seen Miss Carberry on his bed, he shouldn't have let her escape through the window, escape from having more than a cursory appearance in his life.

CHAPTER EIGHTEEN

THE NEXT MORNING, MARGARET strolled to the breakfast room. She may have been up late, but she was not going to spend the morning sleeping, no matter how sumptuous the duke's sheets were.

This was an adventure, something entirely different from her normal life in London, and Margaret did not intend to waste a moment.

The breakfast room overlooked the garden, and for a moment Margaret could only stare at the rows of roses and neatly trimmed hedges. The sun had been absent in England much of the year, but now it was back in full force.

She returned her gaze to the table. Staffordshire china glimmered in the bright light, depicting fanciful scenes of an idyllic England removed from her experiences in London. There'd been nothing romantic about the capital's hack and carriage filled streets.

Margaret didn't miss coach drivers berating the speed of their horses and that of the horses pulling other carriages, and she didn't miss the heavy scents of a crowded city in the summertime. Only the very nicest neighborhoods were in any manner lacking such unpleasantness. She didn't miss needing to take transportation everywhere she went, not because Margaret was in any manner incapable of walking, but because the security risks of wandering about herself were deemed too high.

Margaret wanted to wander through the countryside and hear the sound of the ocean. She liked seeing her friends in London, but she had no desire to live there year-long, like Papa's work demanded.

No. This was a lovely place.

Variously shaped loaves of bread reclined in baskets, and jewel-colored jams and honey sat in crystal bowls.

She stepped into the room, turned her head, then noticed the Duke of Jevington sitting at the head of the long breakfast table.

Her heartbeat quickened, and his lips curled.

Margaret averted her gaze. She didn't need to think about his lips. Or the manner in which light played in his hair. Or his chiseled features.

Margaret rather wished her parents had risen early. Perhaps coming down here by herself hadn't been an intelligent use of her time, after all. Perhaps she'd undervalued London. At least when she was at home her heart didn't beat in an odd manner when she entered a room. Dullness was not devoid of virtue.

"You're alone," the duke said, and for some reason the man's eyes glimmered.

Well, she didn't need to ponder too hard why that was the case.

It was evident he was still apprehensive around her mother, and he had not yet formed a full opinion of her father. Magnates had a habit of being intimidating, even when they delegated all child rearing duties to their spouses.

It could not be that he had any interest in her.

"You're alone as well," Margaret said. "Where are your friends?"

"Horse riding," he said. "I thought I would be a good host and not abandon your family."

"You didn't need to do that."

"Naturally not," he said. "I quite suspect you're familiar with breakfasting, but I can still give you advice."

"Advice?" She raised an eyebrow.

"The marmalade is a must," he said. "Some people might go for the jam, but the marmalade is particularly superb."

"Very well." Margaret smiled, reached for a roll, and spread marmalade over it. She bit into it, conscious of the duke's gaze.

"How do you like it?"

"It's most scrumptious."

The Duke of Jevington's eyes remained on her, then he averted his gaze abruptly. He raked his hand through his hair. "It's a pity there's so little left in the jar. I'm sure your parents and grandmother will want some too."

"Well, they actually prefer jam, but—"

He shook his head and glanced at the sole footman in the room. "Could you please fetch some more marmalade?"

The footman bowed. "Very good, Your Grace."

"Thank you," the duke said cheerfully.

Margaret widened her eyes. "You wanted him to leave."

"You are a very intelligent woman."

She stared at him.

"You needn't act so surprised."

"Did you also want your two bodyguards to haul you away last night?"

The duke's cheeks turned a ruddy color. Somehow, they did not hinder his indisputable handsomeness, rendering him an odd boyish quality.

"I'm—er—sorry about that," he said. "New position. They are liable to be rather over eager in the fulfillment of their duties."

Her lips twitched, and she moved her gaze about the room, lest she linger on the duke.

A large portrait sat on the wall. A family played outside, and it took Margaret a moment to realize that the painting depicted the estate. Judging from the clothes, Margaret imagined that this must be Jasper's family, and she stared at the boy with cherubic curls.

"That's my family," the duke said, and his voice was more serious.

Margaret flushed. "Forgive me, I shouldn't have stared."

"Nonsense, I put the painting here. I want to look at it. There are some other paintings of them in the Painting Gallery, but I moved this here."

"It's a lovely spot for a beautiful painting. They look so happy."

"Yes," the duke said. "That's not just the artist's interpretation. We were."

"I'm sorry they passed away."

"I am as well," the duke said, and his voice had a wistful tone to it.

"I can't imagine what it must have been like to lose all of them at once," Margaret said.

"It was atrocious. But I had the other dukes."

"Friends are important," Margaret said, thinking of her own friends in London. It would be nice to see them again.

"People used to think we were tight at Eton because we were snobby," Jasper said. "But that wasn't it. Unless you're that rare royal duke, if you have the title of duke, it's because your father has died. We were all missing fathers. We—er—had something in common, something more substantial than the fact that we were addressed as 'Your Grace' while most of the *ton's* highest elite were only addressed as 'my lord.'"

"It still must have been difficult," Margaret said.

"It was." Jasper sighed. "I want to remember the past without remembering how it ended. I don't want my family's deaths to be the most important thing about them."

"Of course," Margaret murmured. "I lost a brother."

"I'm so sorry."

"It was in the war. We knew when he left that we might never see him again. And then we didn't." Her voice wobbled at the end, but she forced herself to breathe.

She was conscious of the duke's gaze on her, and energy thrummed through her. She poured tea, added milk, then stirred it with rather more care than the task required.

She rarely spoke of her brother. Speaking of him made her parents sad, but it was nice for Margaret to remember he had in fact existed.

They were silent. Finally, the duke tilted his head. "How did you know about my family's death?"

"Ainsworth told me," Margaret admitted.

"That's what you were discussing on your long walk last night?"

She nodded. "You found our walk long?"

He frowned. "Length is subjective."

"Not when it's a measurement," Margaret said.

The duke rose. "Er—perhaps not." He raked his hand through hair. "I wonder where that marmalade is."

"My apologies, Your Grace." The footman returned to the room, clasping a jar. "I'm afraid it took longer for Cook to find it."

"Ah, thank you," the duke said absentmindedly, passing the jar to Margaret.

"Did you say marmalade?" An unctuous voice sounded, and Margaret stiffened.

Mr. Owens stood before them. A wave of embarrassment moved through Margaret, remembering that she'd extolled Mr. Owens' good qualities to an extent he had not met when she'd seen him at dinner.

Perhaps the duke had been correct in stating that Mr. Owens ardent recommendations on books in different genres had not been entirely a signal of a man devoted to reading with whom one might have long bookish conversations. After all, he'd seemed condescending.

"Are you fond of marmalade, Mr. Owens?" Margaret asked as she removed the lid of the marmalade.

Mr. Owens wrinkled his nose. "I find that marmalade has an abundance of sugar in it. One should examine a recipe before casually slathering it on one's toast." He leaned closer to her. "The recipe for this would appall one. I recommend that a woman of your figure confine herself to more savory spreads."

Margaret swallowed hard, and her cheeks flamed.

She didn't want to look at Mr. Owens. She certainly didn't want to look at the duke.

"It seems you have an answer for everything, Mr. Owens," the duke said in an icy tone. "You are insulting a very fine woman."

Mr. Owens did not flush. Instead, he provided a self-satisfactory smile. "I simply was informing Miss Carberry of the ingredients. She might not be aware."

Margaret shifted in her seat.

"I do make it a point of knowing much about a wide variety of topics," Mr. Owens continued, evidently confusing silence with interest. "Knowledge is so often unappreciated. I am certain you understand, Your Grace."

"Of the dangers of marmalade?" The duke shrugged. "It is my favorite topping for toast. I'd recommended it to Miss Carberry."

"Ah." Mr. Owens face whitened somewhat. "But you, Your Grace, are a man in top form. They call you a paragon, Your Grace."

"They?"

"The *ton*. The *haute société*. The *creme de la creme*."

"Ah. Those who scatter French words liberally, as if the war never happened," the duke said, and even though Margaret had been feeling distraught, she found herself forcing her lips from yielding to a sudden instinct to smile.

Mr. Owens' face whitened.

"Do have a seat, Mr. Owens," Margaret said.

Mr. Owens' eyes jolted from one side of the room to the other, as if wondering whether he might find an excuse to abandon the room so shortly after his arrival. But no helpful guest appeared, and Mr. Owens sighed. He dabbed his forehead with a napkin with the air of a man who has recently climbed a tree after being chased by a lion and is now merely attempting to pass the time while he hopes for the lion to leave.

The duke showed no signs of leaving the room, even though he'd long ago finished his breakfast. Instead, he cast steely eyes in Mr. Owens' direction.

"I wager you are a man without sisters," the duke said thoughtfully.

Mr. Owens raised his chin. "I am an only child."

"Ah." The duke flashed Margaret a smug smile, and something curious seemed to happen to her heart.

Margaret's parents arrived in the room, and the pleasant feeling sailing through her abruptly halted.

"Good morning," the duke said quickly, rising. "Help yourself to everything."

Mr. Owens staggered to his feet and gave a cursory bow.

"Your Grace!" Mama dipped into a low curtsy, as if she were practicing visiting the king, then directed her attention to Mr. Owens.

Papa returned their greeting absent-mindedly, his eyes focused on the array of breakfast foods. They sparkled under the morning's bright light.

There was an awkward silence, and Mama sat down slowly, as if she half-expected the duke to pull her aside at any moment and emit a diatribe.

Mr. Owens coughed and turned to Papa. "Are you enjoying your time in England?"

Papa shrugged. "I'm just working."

Mr. Owens raised his eyebrows. "Working?"

Papa nodded. "Yep. I suppose I can do that here as well as in Scotland."

Mr. Owens' widened his eyes, and he turned to the duke. "Mr. Carberry is *working.*"

The duke nodded with an amused expression on his face. "So I've heard."

Mr. Owens gave a frustrated sigh and turned to Margaret. "He *works.*"

Margaret nodded, trying not to let irritation shine on her face. Mr. Owens seemed to forget that he worked as well, though since his work topics were more intellectual, if vastly less financially rewarding, he might dismiss them as an extension of university.

Margaret was not going to get into an argument about Papa here. Not in front of the duke. Not in front of Papa.

"Mr. Carberry is a successful businessman," the duke said.

"I-I don't understand," Mr. Owens muttered.

"He's a magnate," the duke said.

Mr. Owens scrunched his forehead, and his pallor resembled those of certain women in too tight clothes before they toppled to the floor and had to be revived with smelling salts and the loosening of stays.

"He's still in—er—trade." Mr. Owens whispered, then shot Margaret's parents a guilty look, as if realizing they might hear him, even though they seemed enthralled in the breakfast selection.

"You find trade an unadmirable occupation?" the duke asked. For some reason there was a dangerous glint to his eyes, and Margaret shook her head. There was no point irritating Mr. Owens. A man like that would be reluctant to be dissuaded from his opinions.

"Concerning oneself with money is a poor use for one's mind," Mr. Owens said.

"I highly doubt that," Papa said. "Besides, I can read intellectual journals as well. I simply choose not to do so."

"Of course," Mr. Owens said. "I didn't mean to imply—"

"You merely meant to compare it negatively with being a soldier killing people with regularity, or a bishop?" the duke pressed.

"Er—yes." Mr. Owens raked a hand through his hair. "But it's not polite to speak of this."

"I believe you started this line of thinking," the duke said. "And I am most curious to learn more. I would imagine that obviously landowners wouldn't meet your standard."

Mr. Owens blinked. "I wouldn't say that."

"Because I spend a lot of time running my estates," the duke said. "And I have little patience for reading."

"Oh?" Mr. Owens voice sounded oddly high-pitched, and he removed his handkerchief and patted it against his forehead.

"I imagine Mr. Carberry's income is even higher than mine," the duke said.

"Higher than yours?" Mr. Owens' voice squeaked. His eyes darted about the room, landing on Margaret's. She nodded in confirmation, and Mr. Owens exhaled.

"I don't have an estate like yours," Papa said in a relaxed tone to the duke.

The duke shrugged.

"Though if one does come for sale," Mama said brightly, "we have been looking."

"You're looking to *buy* an estate?" Mr. Owens asked. "Like this?"

"It is rare to find a castle on the market," Mr. Carberry said. "And I wouldn't want to find a place too far away."

"No Cornwall for us," Mrs. Carberry said, and they laughed.

Mr. Owens retained a shocked expression on his face, but he glanced at Margaret with greater frequency.

CHAPTER NINETEEN

JASPER MADE A POINT of liking most people in the world, but despite his years of practiced affability, rendered stronger by his natural instinct toward good-naturedness, Jasper struggled to find much about Mr. Owens to like.

His conspicuous condescension was hardly endearing, and he catastrophically failed at behaving with the gallantry required of a gentleman.

The man was a beast.

Perhaps that was a slight exaggeration. Jasper allowed himself the hyperbole. In this situation, hyperbole was excusable.

Mr. Owens did outwardly resemble a gentleman. Perhaps his attire was not as fitted as some of the other dukes, but his cravat was tied with flourish. If Mr. Owens had tied that knot himself, Jasper would need to congratulate him. It was not every man who could stand before a mirror for as long as it would need to take to tie the knot successful. It was certainly not every man who could do that with Mr. Owens' face.

Still, the man couldn't go about making Miss Carberry feel bad. Making her smile less forceful was hardly the act of a good man.

Jasper was suddenly very glad he'd arranged this festivity for Miss Carberry.

If this was the sort of man Miss Carberry might find on her own, then she needed his help. Each of his friends would make better husbands than this man would. A woman shouldn't be criticized for her choice of reading material or her appearance.

Besides, Miss Carberry's appearance was beautiful.

Mr. Owens was a fool to not see it.

Through the large glass windows, he spied his friends returning. Jasper abandoned the room hastily, though not before shooting Mr. Owens a warning glance. At least Miss Carberry's parents remained there. Relief only came when he saw his friends returning from their morning adventure.

"We missed you," Brightling said.

"Did you?" Jasper flashed an innocent smile. He strode into his drawing room, gesturing for them to takes seats.

"You're not one to give up a morning of riding," Brightling said, before settling onto the chaise-longue.

"All about being a good host."

"Ah, yes," Ainsworth said. "Though tell me, just how did you meet this Carberry family?"

"I met Mrs. Carberry and her daughter at a house party Lord Metcalfe was throwing."

"Well, that's not inappropriate," Ainsworth said, before his brows scrunched together. "This wouldn't be the house party that Lord Metcalfe arranged in order to find a wife?"

Jasper shifted his legs, conscious that his friends were staring at him. Finally, he straightened. "It was indeed the same one."

"Ah. How curious." Ainsworth narrowed his eyes. "Are you courting, Miss Carberry?"

Jasper widened his eyes. "No! Naturally not."

He wondered though what it might be to actually court her, to dance as many dances as he could with her every time he saw her, to know her eyes gleamed because of him. How wonderful it might be to take lengthy strolls in the garden with her and not be torn away hastily. How nice it might be to discuss life, to discuss the future, to learn everything about her.

Ainsworth nodded. "Because you do seem fond of her. All those rose petals when she entered the castle last night. It's the sort of thing a person might deem romantic."

"Perhaps he got into a tiff with his gardener," Brightling said loyally.

Ainsworth smirked. "Is that the reason, Jasper? Should we expect to see upturned flowers and jagged hedges?"

"Er—no." Jasper tapped his fingers against his armchair. The seat might be comfortable, but Jasper twisted and turned in it. "I get along well with my staff."

He'd always thought that people who tormented their staff, who caused them to leave their positions hastily, or who raised their voices at them, to be the very worst sorts of people.

Ainsworth nodded thoughtfully.

"Surely, you don't want to spend this house party speaking of my servants," Jasper said.

"No," Ainsworth admitted, "Though I had expected to spend more time with you."

A wave of guilt moved through Jasper.

He forced himself to gaze up at Ainsworth and smile. "You're right. Let's have a pleasant weekend."

"That sounds good," Ainsworth said, but his eyes remained fixed on Jasper, and Jasper sighed.

Sometimes having intelligent friends could only be described in a single word: exasperating.

He thought he'd halted Ainsworth's thought process, but one could never be certain with a man like Ainsworth. After that dreadful breakfast with Mr. Owens, it was more necessary than ever for Miss Carberry to find a proper husband.

CHAPTER TWENTY

BREAKFAST WAS LESS stimulating once the duke left.

"Are you interested in botany, Miss Carberry?" Mr. Owens said.

"I'm afraid I haven't given much thought to botany," she said.

"Ah." He shook his head gravely. "That is a mistake in a young lady. It is important for every young lady to know about botany."

"You believe so?" Mama asked, and her eyes narrowed slightly.

"Oh, indeed," Mr. Owens said solemnly, nodding with such force that a double chin appeared. "What could be more feminine than flowers?"

"Indeed." A pensive look drifted onto Mama's face.

"And you are an expert on flowers, Mr. Owens?" Papa asked.

Mr. Owens tightened his jaw and stretched his lips cumbersomely. If clocks had smiles, they would resemble Mr. Owens'.

"I can imagine you're quite unfamiliar with flowers. Can anything grow in Scotland, since it's so far north?" Mr. Owens shrugged, obviously assigning his question prematurely to the rhetorical variety.

"I assure you," Margaret said, "that plenty of flowers do grow in Scotland. We know. We have seen them."

"All the same," Mama said, "perhaps Mr. Owens would be kind enough to show you around the garden." She looked at him. "I doubt my dear daughter is aware that flowers extend beyond roses, and I rather suspect she cannot name them."

Margaret flushed. When she'd told Mr. Owens she hadn't given much thought to botany, it had been in the hopes of halting a potentially irritating conversation about pistils and petals.

It seemed she was now going to be subjected to a more intensive discussion.

"Miss Carberry, I will be happy to address the gaps in your knowledge," Mr. Owens said. "I can assure you that my knowledge is irreproachable."

"How splendid for you," Margaret said.

He gave a casual shrug. "You are too kind, Miss Carberry. I am enchanted."

Enchanted?

Margaret drew back.

Mr. Owens rose and extended a hand toward her. "Please, let us go."

Margaret put down a half-eaten piece of toast. She hoped lunch would be served soon. She'd been too nervous to eat much.

She glanced at her mother. "Did you want to join us?" Margaret despised the unfamiliar pleading tone in her voice.

Mama blinked. "Ah, nonsense. What do I need to know about flowers? Besides, we can see you from this room."

Margaret's hope drifted away, abandoning her with the speed of a leopard racing over the plains.

Papa slathered some marmalade onto his toast, and a smile appeared on his face. "This is good. Did you try some, young man?"

"I haven't," Mr. Owens said reluctantly.

Papa shook his head. "You're missing out."

Margaret noticed that Papa didn't pass the marmalade to Mr. Owens. She waited a moment, to see if Papa would add anything else, but when he slathered another piece of toast with marmalade, she rose as well and joined Mr. Owens.

"Have a good time, dear," Mama said. "You better go now. I think it might rain."

Margaret frowned. The sky's cerulean color hardly harbingered rain.

"Hurry," Mama said, and Margaret followed Mr. Owens from the room.

Her heart sank as they walked through the corridor, then left the castle.

She didn't feel more buoyant when they strode outside, even when the warm sunbeams hit her skin, and even when she inhaled the floral fragrance of the nearby flower garden.

The latter scent only made her stiffen.

Oh, well.

She could take a stroll in a garden with him. After all, she hadn't been exactly comfortable in the duke's presence. It was nice to have one's heart move at a more steady pace, and for sweat to no longer spring up spontaneously on the back of her neck as if she'd accidentally worn a woolen dress intended for the coldest days of the year.

Voices sounded from the other side of the hedges, and she peered over, spotting the brim of the duke's top hat. He and his friends were laughing together, and she was reminded of the group of little boys who'd all had in common that their fathers had died. Her heart squeezed, and she was happy they still had one another.

"No need to tarry," Mr. Owens said. "Exercise is good for somebody of your form."

Margaret stiffened.

"You should walk for two hours each day, no excuses," Mr. Owens said. "Forty-five minutes after each meal."

"That's one hundred thirty-five minutes," Margaret said automatically. "That's over two hours."

"Are you certain?" Mr. Owens scrunched up his forehead.

"Yes," Margaret said.

Mr. Owens shrugged. "All the better, then."

"I believe you may have meant forty minutes after each meal," Margaret said.

"Excuse me?"

"Because that would be one hundred twenty minutes."

The man stared at her blankly.

"Two hours, instead of over two," Margaret said quickly.

"Er—right," Mr. Owens said. "So it is. I was perhaps over generous with my recommendation given your—" He waved his hand in her general direction.

Margaret flushed. "Do you walk two hours each day?"

Mr. Owens' eyes widened, then he laughed. "You are amusing. Naturally, I do not walk so much each day. *I* do not need to do so.

"Is there something about me that you would like to say?" Margaret asked sternly.

Mr. Owens raised his eyebrows. "There is. I must say, I'm surprised you asked. So many women are less direct. I do know they are the weaker species, but I am always surprised by just how weak they are."

"Women are not a different *species*," Margaret said.

There was more she wanted to say, but she could at least say that.

Mr. Owens raised his eyebrows. "You are quite pedantic, young lady."

"I want to be correct," Margaret said, but her voice wobbled.

"Well, well. I suppose there is nothing wrong with the urge to flaunt one's intelligence. It is odd we say that children should be seen but not heard. It is a rule some people should not forget." He gave her a significant look. "Besides, there's something more important you should focus on."

"Indeed?" She steadied her jaw, lest her lips scowl.

"Your curves, dear woman, are excessive. I'd hoped I could merely hint, but—" He gave a helpless shrug, "I see you require more clarification."

Margaret inhaled. And exhaled. She clenched and unclenched her fists.

She was not going to lose her temper.

Margaret had lived her entire life without losing her temper. She was hardly going to start on a beautiful day in a beautiful garden by a beautiful castle.

"Mr. Owens, may I remind you that we only met yesterday?"

"It feels like longer."

Margaret's lips twitched. "Ah yes, each minute feels like a year."

Mr. Owens guided her toward a rose bush. "These are—er—pink roses."

Margaret had rather expected his botanical tour would involve more details.

There was an awkward silence, then Mr. Owens descended to the ground. He smoothed his trousers, fluffed his cravat, and moved his right knee forward.

"Are you quite well?" she asked.

She'd thought he must have had a mishap with his boots, but he'd been striding around quite capably before, and it seemed odd he would now struggle so much with them that he would require to adjust them.

The man wasn't looking at his boots though. He was looking at her.

Margaret shifted her legs awkwardly. The ground might be well-maintained, but it was still uneven. No doubt that was the reason her knees buckled slightly.

Mr. Owens looked at her with intensity. It was almost as if—

She shook her head.

Naturally the man was not proposing. That would be impossible. Just because the man had taken her to an elaborate garden, filled with all manner of enchanting flowers and all manner of lovely fragrances, did not mean he was proposing.

That would be absurd.

He'd only just met her. And much of the time had been him criticizing her with various degrees of forcefulness.

No, just because some men chose to kneel while proposing did not mean he was about to express a ridiculous desire for them to entwine their lives together for all eternity.

Mr. Owens cleared his throat. "It is odd, Miss Carberry, that you agreed you had felt as if you had known me for a long time. I have an ambition to know you, in actuality, for a long time."

She'd expected some sort of statement about flower stems, but he'd launched into a speech about time. "I don't understand."

He flashed his patronizing smile. "My dear child, will you agree to spend the remainder of your life with me?"

Margaret stepped back, and a thorn tore against her dress. "I-I don't understand."

"I am asking you to marry me," he said.

"Oh."

He gave an exasperated sigh. "Say yes."

Margaret was silent.

"It's one word," he said.

"This is happening quickly," she said.

"Cupid's arrow is not without speed," he said. "Whoever heard of a slow arrow? Ha!"

Margaret's lips wobbled.

The man had proposed.

He'd actually proposed.

Margaret had never had anyone propose to her before. Even having a man offer to dance with her was a rarity, but this man wanted rather more than a quadrille.

He wanted a marriage.

To her.

Margaret Carberry, wallflower and desperate debutante.

"I need an answer," he said, his knee wobbling.

Right.

Margaret could answer. After all, she knew the correct answer: yes. Her mother had been striving for her to marry someone all year.

Perhaps Mr. Owens was not a duke. Perhaps he was a younger son of a baronet. But he could hardly be termed a dreadful match. *Technically.*

Margaret stared at Mr. Owens.

The man wasn't particularly handsome, but he was at least of an average appearance. Perhaps his features were unremarkable, but they weren't unpleasant.

She had more issues with his character. Reading had always seemed emblematic of a thoughtful person, but Mr. Owens seemed more interested with memorizing facts, with varying degrees of success, and repeating them at moments he deemed opportune.

And yet... how could she say no?

CHAPTER TWENTY-ONE

SOMETHING DISTRACTED Jasper from his chitchat with the other dukes, and he glanced over the hedge. Later he would not be certain whether it was some sixth sense or whether some small animal had nudged him in that direction. Had a bird chirped?

Margaret stood on the other side of the hedge with Mr. Owens. Now that she was not sitting, he could appreciate the manner in which her pale blue dress hugged the curves of her body.

Not that he was looking at her, though it wasn't for lack of beauty.

His focus was on Mr. Owens.

The man knelt.

Mr. Owens did not appear like a man who would spontaneously kneel. He'd shown no interest in the vertebrae that favored ground habitation, and though a lesser man might fall victim to loose laces, Mr. Owens seemed too fastidious to embark into the world without careful checking and double checking of the state of his footwear.

Jasper told himself Mr. Owens might have experienced some cobbler issue that required him to kneel even though a perfectly good bench was nearby. Mr. Owens appeared fastidious, but any man might experience a cobbler issue. That's why cobblers existed after all.

Somehow, Jasper didn't feel reassured.

Jasper strongly suspected the reason for Mr. Owens change of pose, and he didn't require the use of Belmonte's navigation equipment to make his conjecture.

Mr. Owens must be proposing.

Jasper's plan had worked splendidly: Miss Carberry had received a proposal. She wouldn't marry Jasper, and he would be able to spend the rest of his life content that he'd not been forced into marriage.

Jasper had hoped the men's interest might be piqued during the visit, but he'd only dreamed about a proposal. The house party wasn't even finished, and the violinists hadn't had a chance to play their full, romantic repertoire.

Jasper considered shouting to the gardener that a celebratory champagne was essential. He could almost taste the bubbles flitting in his mouth.

And yet, he didn't *feel* happy.

And Jasper mostly felt happy. Not experiencing the emotion was a novel experience. But he was certain his heart never normally ached in such a manner, just as he would have remembered if he normally had a sour taste in his throat. No doubt eating would be a much less pleasurable occupation if that were the case.

"You've grown quite pale," Brightling observed.

"Have I?" Jasper asked.

"Yes." Brightling nodded seriously.

She was happy, Jasper reminded himself.

She'd wanted to spend time with Mr. Owens, and now she was.

This was what accomplishment felt like. If Jasper's heart didn't precisely soar, that most likely had more to do with the fact that Jasper was accustomed to being accomplished.

And yet, the man was dreadful. He was utterly odious. If he married Miss Carberry, he would no doubt take pleasure in belittling her and asserting his authority, meager as it might be. How could Miss Carberry continue her interest in ornithology and birds if her husband would not even permit her to leave the safe confines of his house? How could she do anything at all except display reverence to the man's supposed intelligence and knowledge lest he barrage her with insults? How could she ever relax, knowing that simply reaching for the marmalade might lead to a tirade? To know that no moment was ever truly relaxing? To know she could never fully concentrate on her own interests again?

Women married people like Mr. Owens all the time. He didn't want Miss Carberry to make their mistake. Marriage was not something that could be reversed.

But now Mr. Owens was planning to spend the rest of his life with Miss Carberry.

Jasper bit back a groan. He needed to see what was happening. He turned to Hammett. "Perhaps I'm not feeling so well. I'll just nip back to the castle."

"Morning nap?" Brightling asked dubiously.

"Perhaps!" Jasper said, forcing his voice to sound cheerful.

Unfortunately, Brightling's eyes only narrowed. Perhaps cheerfulness was not something sick people strove to emanate. Perhaps some of them were simply grumpy.

Jasper felt grumpy.

He felt very, very grumpy.

Jasper gave an awkward wave to Brightling, then bounded to the flower garden.

If only his gardeners hadn't made the place look so romantic. How could Miss Carberry do anything but accept Mr. Owens' proposal?

Jasper hurried toward Mr. Owens and Miss Carberry. It was only when he neared them, that he halted.

This didn't have anything to do with him. He had no claim on Miss Carberry. If she wanted to marry Mr. Owens, well, she could do that. After all, yesterday she'd enthused about what they'd had in common.

His heart squeezed for a peculiar reason, and he lingered near the garden.

Mr. Owens remained kneeling.

Shouldn't more have happened now? Shouldn't they be embracing? If a woman had just accepted his offer of marriage, he'd want to kiss her.

Finally, Mr. Owens rose. His facial expression remained the same, and his manner retained their customary stiffness.

There was no embrace.

Then he tramped away, his back stiff, leaving Miss Carberry by the rose bush.

MARGARET'S HEART THUMPED oddly as Mr. Owens moved efficiently through the garden, away from her forever.

The man had proposed.

And she'd rejected him.

At some point she would regret this, but that moment hadn't arrived yet. Her mouth dried all the same. Mr. Owens met all her qualifications for being a good husband. He was intelligent. At least, he was intelligent enough. Perhaps he wasn't particularly kind, but perhaps that was an elusive quality in people. Her mother wasn't particularly kind either.

And yet, when he'd knelt before her, the only question that had occupied her mind was how she could decline gracefully.

Even though she despised living with her parents.

Even though she had no other prospects. The Duke of Jevington might speak optimistically of marrying her off to one of his friends, but she possessed a more realistic appraisal of her qualities. Mr. Owens had been her best hope for marriage, and she'd said no, as if she received offers every day.

Heavens.

What would her friends think? What would her *parents* think?

Her stomach twisted. She wanted to flee to her chamber, but she had no urge to happen upon Mr. Owens as he continued his steady strides away, and she certainly had no urge to encounter her parents. How much might they have seen from the breakfast room?

She ambled toward a stone bench. As she rounded the rose bush, she nearly barreled into the Duke of Jevington.

The man was staring at her with an odd expression on his face, and she shrank back.

"Mr. Octavius Owens proposed to you," he said.

She closed her eyes.

Oh, no.

He'd witnessed it.

"And you said no," the duke said.

She nodded abruptly, not wanting to gaze into his eyes. The man had arranged all of this so she might marry someone... and yet, when she'd received an offer, she'd rejected it.

She could not spend the duration of their conversation staring at a rose bush.

He didn't appear to disapprove of her.

On the contrary.

Something like joy moved through her.

Then the duke extended his hand, and she took it, disoriented.

He leaned nearer her, and the sheer movement caused her heart to spin. The world tilted and swayed, even though Margaret hadn't taken a single step, much less fallen.

But his face appeared larger than before, closer than before.

And in the next moment, his lips brushed against hers.

And in the moment after that, his lips did more than brush against hers. His lips teased hers open, then everything was bliss.

The space between them narrowed. His scent of cotton and lemon drifted over her. She'd never considered the combination intoxicating before, but now it seemed an oddity that none of the smugglers during the wars with France had bottled up that combination.

He placed sturdy hands on her waist, and he stroked her hair, seeming to find wonder in it. The experience should have felt awkward and uncomfortable and perhaps even frightening. Kissing was certainly something she'd never done before, and the appeal had seemed questionable.

But this felt like none of those things. Instead, her heart seemed to have taken up flight as a hobby, because it soared through her.

She glided her hands up gingerly, placing her hands onto his tailcoat. The woolen fabric felt rough, despite the barrier of her gloves, and yet not touching was impossible. He narrowed the distance between them, and a moan fell from his mouth. His chest pressed against her, crushing her bosom, and emotions fluttered through her.

This was what a kiss was like.

This was why everyone spoke of the action with reverence.

But she shouldn't kiss him.

The thought was absurd. If she kissed him here, in the garden, someone might see. Her mother would force him to marry her.

And unlike other people who kissed, then married, he wasn't kissing her because he'd declared he'd loved her. After all, he'd arranged this whole event due to relief at *not* being forced to marry.

No.

If he kissed her, it was to impart some educational knowledge. That had been clear from the outset. She shouldn't develop fanciful notions. Fanciful notions that might arise if she continued to linger on the loveliness of his scent, the strength of his arms, and the touch of his lips.

She pulled away abruptly. "I—I..."

Her mouth felt thick and useless. She wanted to bury herself in his arms again. She wanted him to continue to kiss her, but instead his expression shifted.

CHAPTER TWENTY-TWO

JASPER'S HEART QUAKED, and he stepped away. The task felt momentous, as if he were a magnet who'd managed to separate from his mates. He looked around, as if rather expecting a journalist to appear to write an article about his powers of restraint.

Even now, he longed to clasp Margaret in his arms again. He wanted to feel her warmth and her soft curves. He wanted to run his hands through her thick locks, and he wanted to kiss her lips.

Blast it, he wanted to kiss more than her lips.

He wanted to trail kisses over her throat. He wanted to press his lips against the space where her neck and shoulders met, and he wanted to nibble on the delectable lines of her collar bone.

And then he wanted to explore more.

He craved to kiss her bodice. He yearned to free her of her fichu, toss it from the balcony so it sunk to the bottom of this wretched moat. He wanted to feel more softness, more roundness, more Margaret. He wanted to place his hands on her waist, then do indecent things. Things that involved raising her skirt, things that involved truly *knowing* her, things that a gentleman should not think about with a young lady of a good reputation.

"I—I should go," he said hoarsely.

Hurt flickered across her face.

Blast it, this wasn't the gentlemanly way to leave her.

But it would hardly be gentlemanly to stay with her. Not when he craved to pull her toward him.

He sighed.

He'd always prided himself on having more restraint. He wasn't a schoolboy. He wasn't a student at Cambridge, eager to explore carnal pleasures.

And yet he was certain that even then, even when kisses were new and pleasurable, his heart hadn't soared with that vigor as when kissing her.

Kissing Margaret hadn't been supposed to feel that good. It hadn't been supposed to wrap him in a cozy feeling, as if he were being tucked into a friendly cloud.

Blast it.

He'd been a fool. He hurried outside, farther away from Margaret, and his feet pounded over the grass, neatly trimmed by the flock of sheep kept for that purpose. But then he stopped.

He was behaving idiotically.

He couldn't just kiss a woman, then run away. She must think him completely mad. Or worse, she might think he abandoned her.

He halted his frantic pace.

Dukes of Jevington did not abandon a lady in a garden. No matter how much her presence might make him think of doing all sorts of unspeakable things to her. No matter how much their kiss had shattered him. He jogged back toward the garden. The other dukes saw him and waved.

"Over here, Jevington," Ainsworth called.

"Just popping into the garden for a bit first," Jasper called back.

"Because he destroyed all the roses," Brightling told Ainsworth in an overly loud whisper.

Jasper ignored the curious expressions of his friends and reentered the garden. The soft floral scent and the barrage of beauty was not enough to put him at ease. He needed to get to Margaret.

At once.

JASPER HAD KISSED HER. And it had felt wonderful, as if some pyrotechnic display were happening inside her.

But he hadn't kissed her because he loved her. He hadn't kissed her because he was courting her.

He'd planned this whole spectacular event simply to ensure that she never became entangled with him again.

And now she'd ruined it.

Jasper didn't want to be with her. Jasper was kind and generous and spectacular. He was a paragon of everything good in the world. He didn't need to be tied with her.

Because Margaret might pretend not to hear what the *ton* said about her, but she knew. She'd even heard the servants at home gossip about her, when they didn't think she could hear.

She knew she was different. She struggled to fit in with other debutantes, to take the requisite interest in haberdashery and coiffures. She wasn't good at water coloring, and the thought of running this large house didn't fill her with excitement, but with dread.

No. If Jasper ever decided to marry, he could pick someone else. Someone better. Someone whose parents hadn't forced him to marry. Someone he loved.

Margaret sat back on the bench, lest her feet decide to stop working.

No one had ever kissed her before.

After all, most debutantes hadn't been kissed, even if some of them might speak about certain gardeners and groomsmen at their country estates with delight.

One could hardly go about kissing if one had no intention of marrying. Doing anything but marrying well would be an insult to one's upbringing, the skills of one's governesses, the vigor of one's pastor at preaching on the necessary importance of following one's elders' wishes, no matter how unpleasant, and finally to oneself.

And yet the duke had kissed her. *Jasper* had kissed her.

"Margaret?" Jasper's voice sounded behind her, and her heartbeat quickened, recognizing her given name on his lip.

He approached her rapidly, and despite her earlier worry that her legs might have developed toppling tendencies, she stood.

"I shouldn't have left," he said.

She waited, unsure what he was going to say next. Her heart clenched, and perhaps she couldn't have spoken, even if she knew what to say.

And yet, her body longed for him. It craved him. She yearned to collapse against his strong, sturdy chest. She wanted to lean into his arms, to inhale his scent of cotton and citrus, of utter masculinity.

Even though they'd only kissed briefly, not kissing him now seemed odd and confusing, as if her body thought she were denying it oxygen or some other vital element.

She moved her gaze up from his broad chest, to his slightly rumpled cravat, to his sturdy chin and chiseled cheekbones. His hair curled appealingly, just as it always did, but when she gazed at his eyes, she halted.

His eyes didn't sparkle, and they didn't gleam or shimmer. His eyes appeared solemn, and her heart thudded.

The man may as well have been any man wearing a mask that resembled Jasper. Every limb appeared stiff—she drew back automatically.

"About what happened—" The man glanced nervously around. "Er—perhaps we should speak elsewhere."

She nodded. "My parents are still inside the castle."

"Then—" He looked around, clearly checking whether anyone might be listening. Voices still murmured from the other side of the hedge. "Follow me."

He turned abruptly, and she hastened behind him, unsure where he was leading her. Was he taking her toward the lake? Or merely to another garden? Perhaps the spice one? She could smell the scent of rosemary, but he marched past until they reached the maze.

He rotated and grinned. His shoulders lacked their earlier tension. "No one will find us here. This was my favorite hiding space as a child."

"Your ancestors showed great consideration and forethought."

He chuckled. "Indeed."

They reached the opening of the maze, and for a moment Margaret was distracted by the tall hedges that loomed over her.

"After you," Jasper said, and she stepped inside, her heartbeat thumping.

ALL JASPER HAD ACCOMPLISHED now was scaring her.

Blast it.

Jasper didn't want to scare anyone, least of all Margaret. At some point she'd stopped being Miss Carberry.

"I must apologize," he said, conscious his voice was hoarser than normal.

She jerked her head toward him.

"My emotions..." He swallowed hard. "I shouldn't have kissed you. I'm sorry. It won't happen again."

The last word managed to cause his heart to tighten in an odd manner.

He ignored it.

Perhaps he'd been doing too much running. He'd always considered himself athletic, but he was nearly thirty, and everyone said dreadful things happened at thirty.

He'd supposed they were speaking about marriage, but marriage didn't seem nearly as dreadful as he'd always assumed. Perhaps they were eluding to sprint speeds.

He inhaled the familiar scent of the hedges. The world grew darker, as they proceeded farther into it.

She tensed, and he halted. He refrained from the temptation of simply proceeding farther into the maze, as if they were going for a normal walk, as if he hadn't just kissed her, as if the world hadn't simply changed.

"I have one question," she asked.

"You won't have a baby from the kiss," he said.

Her eyes widened. "N-No. That wasn't the question."

"Oh." He frowned. "Then what is it?"

"Why did you kiss me?" she asked, her voice trembling oddly.

Guilt shot through him. "It was ungentlemanly of me."

"So, you kissed me to be ungentlemanly?" she asked.

His eyes widened. "Nonsense. I kissed you because... I thought you were going to say yes to Mr. Owens. And I was relieved."

"And kissing is your first reaction after relief?"

He stared at her.

He might be a rogue, but he didn't go about embracing women normally.

"No." He frowned and assessed her. "I don't know how I missed you."

"Missed me?"

He nodded. "I should have paid attention to you from the very beginning."

Her cheeks pinkened at his words.

"Oh?" Her voice gave an unladylike squeak, but it didn't matter.

His eyes didn't appear as sober before, and his lips twitched.

"You're quiet," he said. "That's how I missed you."

"Oh?" she murmured.

"Yes," he said, conscious uttering one syllable words hardly counted as conversation, but unable to say anything more. Words were suddenly very complex things.

"May I kiss you again?" he asked.

She nodded

And so, he did.

And he kissed her.

And kissed her.

And kissed her.

Their tongues danced as he swept his arms about her body, drawing her soft curves toward him. He'd kissed women on dozens of moonlit balconies, the sound of musicians wafting toward him, but nothing compared to this experience. His legs quivered, even though his legs hadn't even quivered when hundreds of Frenchmen had charged toward him at Waterloo, bayonets in hand.

He needed *more*. More Margaret. He lay her down on the ground, far from the eyes of anyone. No one would be able to see them.

His valet would wonder what he'd done to his attire when he returned, but it didn't matter.

All that mattered was Margaret.

All that would ever matter was Margaret.

Because Jasper had no intention of abandoning his plan for the house party. He'd hoped to find her a husband, and he had found one: himself.

They could discuss that later, ideally when Jasper was armed with his mother's ring.

For now, they could enjoy the moment.

Life was going to become very wonderful.

CHAPTER TWENTY-THREE

"HEAVENS!"

Margaret's heart quickened, and this time it was not because of the loveliness of Jasper's touch. She recognized the piercing voice.

"My daughter has been compromised!" the voice wailed.

Jasper scrambled up. His face paled, and his smile, which seemed so consistently present, had vanished.

Lily barked and nudged her head against his legs, and he bent and patted her absentmindedly.

Margaret scrambled up from the ground. She smoothed her dress, conscious that leaves clung to it in an indecent manner. Fire swept up the back of her neck and settled onto her cheeks.

Mama turned dramatically to the duke and raised her finger in an accusatory gesture. "You were *kissing* my daughter."

Jasper was silent. His gaze darted about, then Margaret realized more people were here. She stared at the shocked expressions of Jasper's closest friends.

"You are my witnesses," Mama declared. "My poor dear daughter. My *only* daughter. Being taken by this man."

Jasper was always confident, always prepared, but in this position, he was none of those things. His lower lip dropped down, as if he'd decided to impersonate one of the fish that swam in the lake.

Finally, he inhaled. "Mrs. Carberry, I assure you—"

Mama flung her hand up. "Don't 'Mrs. Carberry' me. I know what I saw."

"Your daughter's maidenhood is intact."

Embarrassment moved through Margaret at a faster pace. She didn't want to hear Jasper explain that what they'd done had meant nothing. She didn't want him to claim he didn't need to marry her—that he didn't *want* to marry her—that there was no child on the way.

And so, Margaret ran.

She sprinted down the end of the maze, forcing herself to remember how to exit.

"Margaret!" her mother called. "Come back here!"

Her feet thudded over the padded dirt of the maze, and when she exited it, she continued to run. Her lungs burned, and she had the horrible sense that all manner of leaves and twigs were clinging to her dress. She was ruining the dress, just as she'd ruined everything else.

Jasper was going to be forced to marry her.

She knew that.

She'd seen all the witnesses.

Whatever Jasper's faults, he was a gentleman. He'd try to do the right thing.

Love swept through her. It filled her, it buoyed her. Life was good simply because he existed, and that would have to suffice.

After all, she wasn't going to allow herself to fantasize about a life with him like some silly schoolgirl. She wasn't going to let her mother take her back to Madame Abrial's, this time for a wedding gown. She wasn't going to become the Duchess of Jevington, as if she actually belonged beside him.

No.

He would marry her reluctantly. She'd already heard him attempt to persuade her mother that nothing untoward had occurred. So, she needed to make certain he wasn't forced to marry her.

Jasper was too wonderful to be confined to marry for anything less than for love. Jasper deserved everything.

There'd been one person who hadn't discovered her in the hedge.

One person who might agree to help her.

Her lungs burned, and she couldn't be certain it was simply because of the speed with which she'd reached the manor house, and not because of distaste for her next task.

Time was of the essence, and she refused to waste any. She marched into the castle.

"Good afternoon, Miss Carberry." The butler's voice sounded behind her, surprise evident in it.

"G-Good afternoon."

She hurried up the steps. *He* needed to be in the library.

She strode over the corridor, past the gilt-framed portraits of the duke's ancestors, and past the ornate furniture from his travels. Finally, she pushed open the door to the library.

Mr. Octavius Owens sat at a table. His eyes widened somewhat, and disapproval flickered over his face. "Are you unwell, Miss Carberry?"

"Unwell?" Her voice squeaked.

Whatever she'd expected him to say, she hadn't expected that.

"I'm fine," she said.

"Er—good."

A mirror hung over a sideboard, and she glanced at her reflection, appalled at her unkempt appearance. No wonder he had asked if she was unwell. She patted her hair, but she needed a brush and twenty minutes to devote to it, before she might return it to a respectable state.

She sighed.

Perhaps she should have gone to change her attire. She didn't have time for that. At some point, her mother would be finished scolding the duke for a crime he did not commit, and they would return to the castle.

Margaret needed to be gone before that happened.

But she couldn't do it alone.

"Mr. Owens," she said. "I have a proposition for you."

THIS WAS NOT WHAT JASPER had wanted to happen.

Having Margaret' parents and his best friends encounter him when he was kissing her was dashed embarrassing. It was the sort of mortifying thing that happened to other people.

Not Jasper.

Jasper preferred to give a woman privacy on such occasions. It was the polite thing to do.

Even his married friends didn't go about kissing in front of him. A man had standards, even if he possessed roguish tendencies.

He cleared his throat. That kiss had been bloody good.

It had been everything a kiss should be.

And the fact that they'd discovered him had meant it had been going on for quite a while.

"You'll need to marry her," Mrs. Carberry said, raising her voice to a wail. "We must go to the Archbishop of Canterbury immediately."

Jasper closed his eyes. "Don't you think that's a trifle unnecessary?"

"Absolutely not," Mrs. Carberry said. "You *are* going to marry my daughter."

He sighed.

Margaret deserved more than a hasty wedding in Canterbury. Kent wasn't exactly near Dorset, and he didn't want to show up at the Archbishop of Canterbury's rooms without warning. That was the sort of thing that would assure scowls from the archbishop every time they saw each other. Jasper might not be particularly religious, but this didn't seem the cleverest way to go about doing things.

Not to speak of the fact that special licenses were expensive. If he wanted to give Margaret a good wedding, he'd much rather spend that money on catering for the wedding breakfast. Oysters for everyone. And Chef Parfait could do some of his sugary concoctions that everyone adored. He could marry Margaret at St. George's in London, or if she preferred, at the village church here.

Because there was one thing Mrs. Carberry was absolutely correct in: he was going to marry Margaret. He was going to make her his wife, and he was going to make her very, very happy.

And he had the delightful feeling that she was going to make him very happy as well.

"I don't think Jevington was *literally* defiling her," Hammett said loyally.

"And she didn't *look* upset," Brightling added, in what Jasper hoped was an attempt at assisting him, because Jasper certainly didn't desire to imagine his friends *watching* and assessing their respective enjoyment levels.

"Of course, Margaret enjoyed it," Jasper exclaimed. "The whole point of pleasure making is to create pleasure. Any idiot knows that. If some poor souls are flummoxed at how to create pleasure, well, that is sad, but I do not fall into that category of unfortunates."

Ainsworth coughed, and Jasper's cheeks heated.

"Are you smiling?" Mrs. Carberry shrieked to her husband. "Men are beasts!"

"I can assure you that animals do not have smiling abilities," Mr. Carberry said.

Mrs. Carberry turned to her husband. "That's your contribution to this conversation? Of all the things you could say, you choose to say *that*?"

"Er—yes," Mr. Carberry said uncertainly. He raised his chin. "It is important to not be lax in the facts, my dear. Details are important."

Mrs. Carberry rolled her eyes. "Right. That's how you became rich."

"Well, it wouldn't have happened with a lackadaisical approach to ledgers," Mr. Carberry said stiffly. He bore the peeved look of a schoolmaster at the end of term who has realized that his students not only have not learned anything, but that they also failed to respect him despite his obvious mastery of bewildering formulae.

"We are not speaking about you," Mrs. Carberry said. "We are speaking about how your darling daughter has been ruined by a *duke*."

Mrs. Carberry did not precisely wink, but the stress on Jasper's position was unmistakable.

Margaret didn't deserve to have her marriage start in this manner. No woman did. Mrs. Carberry shouldn't be speaking so openly about how her daughter had been compromised. That was the sort of thing gossips might choose to chitchat about when they tired of their normal rotation of topics.

If Margaret was going to be his duchess—his wife—she shouldn't think it was just because her dog had powerful nostrils and had dragged her parents there in an innocent attempt for attention. She should think he chose her because he loved her, not because of convenience and threats from her parents. Even the most terrifying matchmaking mamas in the *ton* normally adopted a milder approach to marriage.

Because Jasper did love her.

He would always love her.

He was hers, on this day and forever.

Perhaps he'd only realized it when they'd been kissing, but that didn't make the revelation less powerful, less true.

He sighed. He didn't want to think about what Margaret must be thinking now. He turned to find her, then frowned. "Where *is* Margaret?"

CHAPTER TWENTY-FOUR

MARGARET'S HEARTBEAT hammered, and her chest squeezed. She opened her mouth to speak, but the effort evidently required superhuman strength, for nothing came out. She had the horrible sense her eyes were bulging, and that her face had adopted an unflattering pallor that only appeared during occasions of stress.

"Miss Carberry?" Mr. Owens glanced about the room, as if searching for the bell pull.

She straightened her shoulders.

He was not going to usher in any servants.

He was going to assist her, and he was going to be happy about it.

She cleared her throat. "Mr. Owens, though we have not known each other for long, I confess I have noticed that we have certain mutual interests. Books, for instance. And er—indoor pursuits."

In truth, her favorite things to do this weekend had been outdoor pursuits, but now was not the time to linger on that.

He narrowed his eyes. "I am not a Jonathan Swift devotee."

"Er—yes. I meant books in the general sense."

He nodded, retaining a suspicious gaze.

"Circumstances have—er—occurred, and I find myself in immediate need of a husband."

"Every young lady is in immediate need of a husband," he said.

"Perhaps," she squeaked. "I hadn't thought of that."

Now was not the time to disagree with him.

He gave her a patient smile. "My dear child, it is a pity that intelligence is not evenly distributed between man and woman. It is not your fault though."

Heavens.

She'd thought Mr. Owens perfect when she'd first met him. The mere fact that he'd been in a library had seemed a cause for approval. Even his imperfect physique, which reminded her of her own, had made her feel safe. She'd been suspicious of anyone unlike her.

She wavered.

For one moment.

One moment in which she wanted to leave the library and wait for everyone to return.

But then she remembered Jasper's expression when her parents and his friends had discovered them. She remembered the paleness of his face, the odd tremor in his otherwise sturdy jaw, and his protestations.

No.

She wasn't going to condemn him to a fate he didn't desire.

She assessed Mr. Owens. Perhaps this man didn't make her heartbeat quicken, but quickening hearts weren't practical.

"Before I say something," she said, "you should know I don't intend to love you."

The man's eyes widened.

Perhaps she hadn't broached the subject with sufficient delicacy.

Fiddle-faddle. She hadn't been taught to say such things.

And yet, he was her only hope, and she needed to ask him. She needed to rescue Jasper from an unwanted marriage.

"Nevertheless," she continued, "I believe that we are not entirely unsuited for each other."

"Do you have a point?" he asked. His visage had darkened, and his eyes, that had seemed mostly neutral, if not precisely genial, had a distinct moody edge. It was the sort of look one wouldn't want to encounter in a dark alleyway. Thankfully, they were in a reasonably well-lit library, and she thought he would like what she would say next.

After all, Papa was not exactly poor.

"I have reconsidered your offer from earlier. I would like to marry you," she said quickly.

The man looked appalled.

"You're proposing to me?" Mr. Owens asked finally.

"Er—yes."

It was too late to take the words back, and she needed to remember that the reason why she'd said the words in the first place—Jasper's happiness—had not changed. She rather wished though that Daisy were here. She would like to confer with her.

"So, what do you say?" she asked.

Mr. Owens was silent.

Not good.

"I do have a dowry of course. It's—er—rather sizable. People think it's not large because my parents aren't like the other parents here, but it's—er—pretty big."

"Your father is in industry." Mr. Owens face contorted.

Why did people's faces always do that when they spoke of her father? Perhaps he wasn't the youngest son of a baronet, but he'd done more than any of those sons had ever done. More than go to war and spend the rest of his time prancing about in a uniform. More than becoming a bishop and patronizing everyone with his supposed words of wisdom.

"He's in industry, yes," she confirmed.

Mr. Owens didn't blush, but he did avert his eyes. Margaret took that as a triumph. But she didn't have time to celebrate it.

"I don't think it's appropriate for a woman to ask a man to marry him," Mr. Owens said finally. "Not something I would care to share with others."

"For goodness' sake." Margaret quelled the instinct to roll her eyes. "You propose to me again in that case. And then we'll have to leave."

"I hope you're not suggesting a hasty wedding," Mr. Owens said. "It's not appropriate."

Margaret chewed on her bottom lip. "Did you truly have so many people you wanted to invite to your wedding?"

Mr. Owens was silent. He gave her a wounded look and pressed his lips together. She suspected that if they were married, he would not be so restrained in his commentary.

"So, you're proposing we *elope?*" he said finally. "That we depart in the most scandalous manner possible? And then we spend the rest of our lives together, even though, as you said, we are not in love?"

Margaret's lower lip wobbled.

He was correct. The idea was mad. The only thing she'd accomplished was to horrify him and make her demeanor seem tawdrier. What sort of woman went about proposing to men she barely knew?

"I-I'm sorry." Her voice trembled. "I shouldn't have asked you."

He shrugged. "No, no. I'm just making certain I understand everything. Normally, being in love is a requirement for eloping couples. The process is so foolish."

Margaret swallowed hard. "Of course. And if you marry me, you wouldn't be able to marry someone to whom you were more suited. I shouldn't have asked you."

"Nonsense. You think I believe in such sentimental drivel?" He shook his head. "Women's novels. An entirely abhorrent influence on the weaker sex. Come now, child. There is nothing to worry about. I will marry you."

This was when Margaret's heart should have been soaring, but instead it felt tighter in her chest, as if it had turned to glass and might easily shatter.

Her plan had worked.

"Because of the money?" she asked.

"That helps. Besides, like you said, I don't think I was expecting to marry anyone better, and this saves me the trouble of courting. Women can be quite demanding. All those visits to a girl's parents' house with conversations that last as long as it takes to empty a teapot."

She turned to him. "In that case, we'll need to act now."

"Right." The man frowned with the air of someone who has hitherto prided himself on taking his time, and now is required to hurry and must imagine what that process looks like.

Mr. Owens touched his cravat, and she gritted her teeth. Ensuring he had a straight cravat was not an essential part of the elopement process.

"Please," she implored. "Once they return from the garden—"

He sighed. "Go upstairs, bring as much attire as you can as quickly as you can. I'm not going to wait for some modiste to make new clothes for you. Then come down. I'll tell the footman that I need my carriage. I hope he can get hold of my groom quickly. I've been using the Duke of Jevington's valet, so at least I won't have to wait for him. Understand?"

Her shoulders sank in relief. This was happening. This was good.

"Now do not tarry," Mr. Owens said, "or there will be much explaining to do."

Margaret turned and rushed from the room. She sprinted up the stairs, quickly found her room and began to pile clothes into her suitcase. Her fingers shook, and she wished she had her maid to help her. No doubt she was assisting the servants here.

"Margaret?" Juliet stared at her. An odd expression drifted onto her friend's face. "Are you quite well?"

"Naturally," Margaret said, blinking rapidly. She refused to cry.

Juliet drew her eyebrows together with the knowing air of a governess who suspected a frog, temporarily masked by papers, might be hopping on her desk.

"What's wrong?" Juliet asked sternly.

"Nothing!" Margaret squeaked. She continued to throw clothes into her valise.

"Should I ring for the maid?" Juliet asked.

"There's no time," Margaret said. "The thing is—I'm eloping."

Juliet's eyes goggled. "With whom?"

"A Mr. Owens," Margaret said.

"Where does he live?"

Margaret scrunched her forehead. "I forgot to ask him. Well, there will be much to learn about him on our journey to Gretna Green."

"You mustn't do it," Juliet said. "I haven't heard you mention this man. You can't love him."

"I'm not you," Margaret said. "I have fewer options."

"Just because a man proposes, doesn't mean you need to accept," Juliet said.

"I didn't. Not at first," Margaret said. "I—er—just told him I changed my mind."

"So you mean to travel alone with this man to Gretna Green?"

"Yes?"

"Travel for over a week alone?"

"Yes." Margaret nodded rapidly.

Juliet sighed. "I'm coming with you."

"But you mustn't!" Margaret exclaimed.

"You won't be married. You require a chaperone."

"But you're unmarried. Your reputation—"

"I'm betrothed," Juliet said. "Besides, you're more important."

Margaret blinked, stunned.

Juliet tossed her hair, proceeded to drop her clothes into Margaret's valise. "I'm ready."

"G-Good."

Juliet smiled, opened the door, and Margaret then rushed back downstairs, hauling her luggage with her. She'd packed lightly, despite Mr. Owens' words. There were only so many ball gowns one could wear when eloping.

"Miss Carberry!" The butler uttered a startled cry. "What are you doing?"

Fiddle-faddle. "Just—er—bringing this valise to put in Mr. Owens' carriage."

The butler furrowed his brow. "Mr. Owens tasked *you* to carry one of *his* valises?"

The statement was absurd, but Margaret forced herself to smile. "Just from the landing. I'm afraid I—er—took the initiative. It's really not important."

"A helpful person. Hmph." The butler firmed his lips. "We have footmen for that."

He snapped his fingers, and a footman appeared from an adjoining room.

"Carlson, see that Mr. Owens' valise is placed in his carriage," the butler said. He then turned back to Margaret. "I was not aware Mr. Owens was leaving."

"I do not believe Mr. Owens had planned to leave so early," Margaret said, and the butler inclined his head, evidently accepting her statement.

Mr. Owens proceeded down the steps as the footman returned inside. Relief swept through Margaret. No more awkwardness with the butler.

"Ah, another valise, Mr. Owens?" the butler asked.

"Quite," Mr. Owens said with an unctuous smile.

The marriage would be fine. He was in possession of a modicum of intelligence. Nevertheless, happiness didn't exactly thrum through Margaret.

She wondered when it finally would.

Mr. Owens opened the door for her, and Margaret scrambled inside the carriage. Mr. Owens followed her and settled onto the seat opposite. Then Juliet slid in beside Margaret.

"Who are you?" Mr. Owens stammered.

"I am Lady Juliet," Juliet said. "Miss Carberry's chaperone."

Mr. Owens' mouth fell.

The driver opened the latch. "Are you ready?"

"Yes, indeed," Mr. Owens managed to say.

"Very well, sir," the driver said, and in the next moment, the carriage moved.

Too late, Margaret realized it was customary for a woman in her situation to write a note. Her mother would be confused.

CHAPTER TWENTY-FIVE

JASPER GAZED AROUND the maze. His friends were there, Margaret's parents were there, and Lily was there.

Margaret however was not.

"Margaret is gone," Jasper said.

"I don't think it's proper for you to refer to her by her given name," Mrs. Carberry said primly.

Jasper inhaled.

They'd been in this bloody maze for too long.

He sighed. "Let's return to the castle."

Mrs. Carberry narrowed her eyes. "I hope you're not trying to avoid this conversation."

"Naturally not," Jasper said, striving to keep his voice calm.

Because as tempting as it might be to tell Mrs. Carberry her flaws, she was going to be his mother-in-law. In fact, even though Jasper would have liked to have this discussion in a different manner, perhaps he should inform her.

"Mrs. Carberry, Mr. Carberry." He inclined his head to each of them. He'd thought he might feel awkward, his throat might dry, and his chest might tighten. After all, he'd always thought marriage something to be wary of, categorized similarly to unfamiliar mushrooms and coastal walks in the dark. But he wasn't feeling nervous now. The rest of his life was going to begin soon, and it was going to be glorious. "I am going to marry your daughter."

Mrs. Carberry opened her mouth, then closed it. She shot a glance at her husband, as if fearing her hearing might have decided to fail her at this moment and usher in new words and phrases instead.

"E-Excuse me?" Mrs. Carberry asked finally.

Mr. Carberry beamed. "We're going to get a son-in-law."

"You certainly are," Jasper said.

"I-I don't understand," Mrs. Carberry said.

"Perhaps my friend spoke too hastily," Ainsworth said, joining him hastily.

"I did not speak too hastily," Jasper said.

"B-But you protested," Mrs. Carberry stammered before evidently realizing she was not exactly helping her cause.

"I did not defile your daughter," Jasper said. "We kissed."

"But you'll still marry her?" Mr. Carberry asked, awe in his voice.

"Yes."

Mr. Carberry widened his eyes.

"Now can we please return to the castle?" Jasper said impatiently, before Mr. Carberry might begin musing over his courtship of Mrs. Carberry. "I would like to formally propose to your daughter. I don't know what she's thinking now."

Mrs. Carberry paled. "You're correct. Let's go."

She marched forward, though soon returned with a sheepish expression on her face. "It seems that this is not the correct way."

"Mazes are tricky," Mr. Carberry remarked. "Just a place to send guests to when you don't want to see them for a while."

"We are all leaving." Jasper turned to Lily. "Come, Lily."

Lily wagged her tail and accompanied the others. They strode forward, came to a fork, then shot Jasper puzzled expressions.

Jasper raked his hand through his hair. He rather wished he'd spent more time entering and exiting the maze. He'd been so intent on finding a spot to be hidden with Margaret that he hadn't paid sufficient attention on which route they'd taken.

"I think it's this way," Jasper said, choosing the path to the right.

It was not.

Finally, they exited the maze, and Jasper's heart soared when the castle came into view.

He'd told them.

It was settled.

The rest of his life was truly going to begin soon.

Margaret would be surprised of course. He smiled, looking forward to proposing.

He wished he hadn't torn apart quite so many roses the other night. They would have come quite in handy now. The musicians were scheduled to return in the evening. He wondered whether he might postpone the proposal until then.

He sighed. If only Margaret and he hadn't been discovered. Romance took rather more time than he thought Margaret's parents were willing to allot.

"Good afternoon, Powell," Jasper told his butler as he entered the house.

"Good afternoon, Your Grace," the butler said in a customary solemnity. His voice boomed in its consistently deep baritone, but his eyes flickered in a manner that was less customary, and Jasper halted.

"Is everything well, Powell?" Jasper asked. No doubt Powell had seen an upset looking Margaret enter the house. Undoubtedly the man's gentle nature would be disturbed.

"I'm afraid Mr. Owens and Miss Carberry and Lady Juliet are—er—" He glanced at the others.

"Do proceed, Powell," Jasper said. "No point prolonging it."

"This isn't the theater," Mrs. Carberry said, managing to be unhelpful. At least she was acting in a consistent manner.

"Well, they're gone," Powell said finally. "Miss Carberry was helping Mr. Owens with a trunk. Naturally, I had a footman assist her, but I'm afraid the footman said she got into his carriage. Lady Juliet has also vanished."

An unsettled feeling started in Jasper's stomach. Why would Margaret have left with Mr. Owens?

"And where is the carriage now?" Mr. Carberry's eyes flashed in a manner Jasper was unaccustomed to seeing.

Powell shrugged. "I'm afraid I do not know."

"No doubt they were pleasure riding." Mrs. Carberry shot a worried look at Jasper, as if he might renege on his proposal so quickly.

It would take much more for Jasper to retract his offer of marriage.

"I find it highly unlikely my daughter would go pleasure riding with a man she hardly knows. She shouldn't go pleasure riding with *any* man. Even with her friend." Mr. Carberry turned quickly to Powell with the air of an inspector. "Was

Mr. Owens' carriage a pleasure riding vehicle? Was it a—er—curricle? Or something of that nature?"

Powell's eyes rounded, and he shook his head solemnly. "I'm afraid not, sir. I'm so sorry. I—er—should have stopped her. I didn't know she intended to get into the vehicle."

"It's not your fault," Jasper said quickly. "You didn't know."

Powell nodded. "But all the same, I'm sorry."

Jasper was sorry too.

What on earth was Margaret thinking, going off with this Mr. Owens? The man was utterly unremarkable.

And yet...

Jasper remembered how Margaret had first spoken of Mr. Owens. Somehow, Margaret had managed to think him remarkable. Perhaps, despite everything, she favored Mr. Owens.

Because of Mr. Owens' intelligence.

The thought leaped into his mind and clutched hold of it.

Jasper hadn't thought Mr. Owens to be particularly intelligent, but perhaps that had simply been because of Jasper's own lack of understanding of the topics that Mr. Owens enthused about.

His heart hammered. Perhaps the reason she'd run away was because she knew her mother would insist she marry Jasper. Margaret had protested against her mother's allegations as well. He had thought Margaret was being overly polite, but perhaps he was wrong. Perhaps she'd desperately wanted not to be forced into a marriage with Jasper.

All of a sudden, Jasper's legs jolted as if they'd been replaced with some newborn calf's.

She'd left.

She'd vanished from his life, taking off with a practical stranger who had no castle, no title and possessed no handsomeness, rather than marry him.

He stared at the others, but their expressions had turned to sympathy.

Blast it.

When had he last seen Hammett looking sympathetic? The man was happiest smashing his fist into people's faces.

"Wait!" Mr. Carberry scrunched up his face. "Are we saying that my darling daughter, my sweet, innocent girl, who has never given me a moment of trouble in the past, has run off with Mr. Owens? When she was minutes before kissing the Duke of Jevington?"

"That sounds correct," the Duke of Brightling said politely.

Had Jasper been in less agony, he might have shot Brightling an irritated look. Instead, he only groaned.

Because Brightling was right.

That was what had happened.

He'd declared his love for this woman before her parents, and his friends, and it hadn't mattered. He'd always scoffed at the notion of marriage, but he hadn't considered that it might be beyond his capabilities to achieve.

Margaret had heard her mother speak of marriage.

She would have known if she'd stayed, they would marry.

And yet, she'd chosen to flee.

Away from him.

Forever.

CHAPTER TWENTY-SIX

MARGARET HADN'T MADE a mistake.

That was impossible.

Margaret excelled at all her lessons and she was not one to make a miscalculation. No one would say Margaret acted impulsively this time. The impulsive act Margaret had made was to reject Mr. Owens' proposal in the first place.

Obviously, fleeing from the charming, dashing duke who'd had such regret that when he'd first kissed her, he'd fled, was not a mistake. No doubt the duke thought her parents had been following him the entire time, waiting for a moment to force him to take her as his duchess, even though no one could be less qualified.

Other women might become duchesses, but not Margaret.

She was more suited to become a Mrs. Owens. Her betrothed enjoyed reading, and she would let him. Perhaps occasionally he would offer her condescending suggestions, and she would merely smile and listen. In some cases, a smile would not even be required, depending on the gravity of the information Mr. Owens was imparting.

No, this plan was going well, just as all of Margaret's plans went.

Perhaps her heart ached, and perhaps she might always wonder what might have happened had she stayed, but this was for the best.

She'd been lucky Mr. Owens had expressed an interest in marrying her.

Perhaps their married life would be more pleasant if she'd accepted straight away, but one couldn't change the past. She would simply have to make certain Mr. Owens was content.

Still, as the carriage continued away from the castle, Margaret's confidence wavered.

"Do you prefer going to Gretna Green or Guernsey to elope?" Mr. Owens asked.

"Oh." Margaret straightened. "Guernsey is a possibility? I've never sailed on the ocean."

Mr. Owens gave an exasperated sigh. "The question was meant to be rhetorical. Obviously, Gretna Green is the only proper choice."

"It is?" she squeaked.

Mr. Owens nodded gravely. "It's the traditional choice. When in doubt, always choose tradition."

"Oh. I see."

He smiled. "You do have potential, dear lady."

Margaret's lips tightened. "You do not find it dispiriting to marry in a blacksmith's shop?"

"There is nothing about this journey that is not dispiriting. But at least visiting Scotland will not put us in danger of drowning in the channel."

Margaret nodded, but for the first time she considered that this journey *was* dangerous. Perhaps they might not be shipwrecked, but they still risked their carriage crashing or being accosted by highwaymen. Not to speak of the unsavory men who might be rampant in posting inns.

Mr. Owens glanced at Juliet. "I did not anticipate a woman of your importance would be on this journey."

"Here I am," Juliet said, flashing him a bland smile.

"And you're certain you want to accompany us on the entire journey?" Mr. Owens asked. "Perhaps you would prefer us to drop you in London."

"Nonsense," Juliet said.

Mr. Owens paled. "It will be an—er—pleasure to have you here. But your father—"

"—will be upset when I return," Lady Juliet said.

"So you must make the journey quick." Margaret settled back into her seat, not exactly content but grateful she'd insisted on those things. She refused to remain the timid woman that she'd always been.

The coach continued on its journey, and the spaces between the houses gradually narrowed, until they were in the city, and the coach slowed, inching along.

JASPER RETREATED FROM the worried looks of his friends.

They pitied him.

They weren't supposed to pity him.

The worst thing was that he didn't care. Though he'd always considered himself to possess abundant resources of pride, he wasn't thinking of it now. He wasn't going to continue this house party as normal. He wouldn't feign indifference toward Margaret.

He turned to the musicians. "Play sad music."

"Not quadrilles?"

He shook his head furiously. "Something distressing. Something Germanic."

The musicians conferred shortly, then played something with an appropriate amount of melodrama. Jasper listened satisfactorily as the music leaped from high to low notes, making full use of the violinists' capabilities.

"Good," Jasper said. This might be his moment of utmost sadness, but he was not going to refrain from encouraging his staff, even if they were the temporary sort.

He looked around the corridor at the shocked faces of his friends. He cleared his throat. "The castle and grounds are at your disposal. Perhaps you would care to hunt or—er—play pall mall."

"We're not going to play pall mall," Ainsworth said.

Jasper shrugged. "Naturally. Choose something less childlike. Perhaps you'd prefer to fence. My ancestors' swords are hanging in the dining room."

Ainsworth and the others exchanged glances, and Jasper withheld a groan.

He turned to the musicians. "Come."

The musicians followed him as he marched from the corridor into the library. He didn't want to imagine Mr. Owens and Margaret meeting here, but this whole castle would now be filled with memories of Margaret. Perhaps in a few months he'd meet her at a ball.

If she decided to attend balls.

No doubt Mr. Owens would ensconce her in the country somewhere. He settled himself into the darkest corner of the already dim library.

Yes. This felt appropriately dispiriting.

"Jevington," Ainsworth said gently.

He turned toward his friend's voice and glared when he saw everyone standing there.

"You followed me?" Jasper employed his most outraged tone and raised his eyebrow.

His friends didn't flinch.

Blast them.

"Jevington," Ainsworth said again. "I didn't know that you—er—cared for this woman."

"It is a novel experience for me as well," Jasper admitted.

"Yes, I did think even you would know that the best way to court a woman is not to throw her at other men," Ainsworth said.

"I was not throwing her at anyone," Jasper said, retaining his outraged tone easily.

"Perhaps not literally," Brightling said.

"But you did scatter rose petals about when she entered with me," Ainsworth said.

"And I believe you just had one dance with her last night," Hammett said. "All of us had more."

"Do you have a point? Are you calling in question my courtship abilities?"

"On the contrary," Ainsworth said.

"Well, she didn't have to run away," Jasper said. "And she didn't have to run away with that man." He grimaced.

"Mr. Owens is hardly the ideal man," Hammett admitted.

"Well, I tried telling that to her. I thought she'd listened. She'd just rejected his proposal."

"So, you were celebrating in the maze?" Brightling asked.

Jasper frowned. "Something like that."

"What was the true reason that you invited her here?" Ainsworth asked.

Jasper sighed. "It's not important."

"Are you certain?"

Jasper shook his head. Everything about Margaret was important. If he didn't speak about her now, perhaps he'd never speak about her.

"Her mother attempted to stage a compromising," Jasper said.

"I'm not familiar with that phrase," Ainsworth said, obviously perturbed. Ainsworth was familiar with most phrases, even those in foreign languages.

"Mrs. Carberry tied her daughter to my bed during my most recent ball. Fortunately, she escaped. And because I was grateful, I thought I might make certain to find her another husband."

Hammett blinked. "Mr. Owens?"

Jasper sighed. "I was hoping for one of you. She is wonderful. She'd make someone a wonderful wife."

She was supposed to make *him* a wonderful wife.

"So, Miss Carberry knew you were so desperate *not* to marry her that you arranged a whole house party to find her a husband?" Ainsworth asked.

"Er—yes."

"Is it possible she does not know you might not be entirely horrified at the thought of marrying her?"

Jasper shifted his legs, and Ainsworth got that triumphal look that had been so irritating at Eton.

"Perhaps," Jasper said softly.

"Then you must go after her," Ainsworth said.

CHAPTER TWENTY-SEVEN

THE TRIP HAD BEEN EXCITING at parts, when the coach had climbed through scenic countryside, but mostly it had been tiring.

It was tiring to be cramped in a small space, wedged beside Juliet and the carriage door, and it was tiring as the coach swerved from bend to bend. The unpredictable rhythm made sleep difficult, even though each morning she was exhausted, after a night of sleeping above a busy posting inn. Most of all it was tiring to sit opposite Mr. Owens.

Finally, they arrived in Gretna Green. Margaret exited the carriage.

Happy couples wandered around the village, either blissfully celebrating their first days of marriage or anticipating them. Some of the brides already had rounded bellies, making it clear why they'd needed to elope instead of waiting for the banns to be read.

Margaret stepped forward. Her feet sagged into the muddy ground, and she stared at all the people. She smoothed her dress, and a wave of nervousness came through her.

She was here.

It was truly happening.

She was going to marry Mr. Owens.

She glanced at him. He patted his forehead. No doubt he was still queasy from the journey. Reading wasn't an activity that was well suited to travel, and he'd attempted to read the entire time.

"We're here," he said.

"Splendid!" she said faintly, even though this didn't seem splendid. It seemed the end of her previous life.

Still, she had to marry him.

Mr. Owens produced a faint smile. She hoped he was thinking of possibly happy decades ahead with her, and not simply of the money that her father would give him.

Perhaps it didn't matter.

She raised her chin. "Shall we find a posting inn?"

"We can marry directly." Mr. Owens glanced in the direction of one of the blacksmiths shops.

Of course.

This was what they'd planned to do. A strange quiver moved through Margaret's spine. This was not simply another day. This would be the first day of their marriage, the first day of the rest of her life. This evening would be her wedding night.

A sour taste invaded her throat.

She wasn't ready for this.

"I will need to prepare for the wedding," Margaret said. "I cannot appear like this."

"Hmph." Mr. Owens gazed at her. "You require miracle workers." He shrugged. "I suppose we could wait one more night."

"G-Good," she said.

Mr. Owens offered her his arm, and they proceeded to the nearest inn.

JASPER PACED GRETNA Green. He'd become incredibly familiar with the town in the past few days. The only thing worse than spending the week in a town devoted to weddings was to spend it without the woman he wanted to marry. Every new exclamation of jubilation after a short arrival was not only a sign of the blacksmiths' remarkable efficiency, but at the absolute necessity of spotting Margaret arrive in time.

At least, he hoped he hadn't missed her.

Perhaps her absence signified that she'd changed her mind about the wedding, but maybe it had simply meant something dreadful had happened to delay them.

Jasper, after all, knew all about carriage accidents.

He peered at the incessant stream of carriages. Even regular tourists, with no plans to marry, seemed to pass through here, gawking at the various blacksmith shops.

A woman appeared on the other side of the street accompanied by two maids. Her nose swooped up in the same manner as Margaret's. Was it her? He rushed toward her but was stopped by the traffic.

When he crossed the street, she had gone, presumably into the nearby posting inn.

Well, he was going to speak with her.

He gritted his teeth and stepped into the inn. He marched inside, wishing that not quite so many patrons had decided to crowd into the public house portion. Someone was playing the piano, and other patrons were singing. The innkeepers gave him a wary glance. He'd already inquired whether Margaret and Mr. Owens were here multiple times before.

He ignored the innkeepers and scoured the rooms. Unfortunately, he didn't see them. He ordered a drink and sat at the table. When they came down, he would be here.

The bar maid brought him some ale, though neither the bubbles nor the familiar sour taste distracted him from his view of the door.

Finally, Mr. Owens appeared.

Jasper grinned and rose.

Mr. Owens headed toward the bar, no doubt to order a drink, but when he saw Jasper, his eyes rounded, and he halted abruptly.

"Good afternoon, Mr. Owens," Jasper said.

Mr. Owens gave him a sullen glance.

"Is Miss Carberry traveling with you by any chance?"

"I think you know the answer."

At least this was good. She was here.

His heart soared.

"May I speak with her?"

"No," Mr. Owens said.

"No?" Jasper widened his eyes. "But you don't love her."

Mr. Owens shrugged. "What is love?"

"What is love? Love is the most wonderful thing imaginable. And the most thrilling. And the most dangerous."

"She *wanted* to marry me."

"But she wants to marry me more," Jasper said. "She loves me."

"Did she tell you that?" Mr. Owens asked.

Jasper blinked. "Not in those precise words."

"It's three words," Mr. Owens said pedantically. "It doesn't take long to say."

"Did she tell you she loved you?" Jasper asked.

Mr. Owens hesitated, but then he moved his chin outward, as if it were a cannon he was directing at an enemy ship. "Yes."

Oh.

This wasn't what was supposed to happen.

Jasper was supposed to arrive in Gretna Green, tell Margaret he loved her, then marry her at the blacksmith's shop himself.

He'd worried about not getting to Gretna Green in time, but after the first shock of her disappearance, he'd not worried that Margaret might not accept him. He certainly hadn't thought he might not even *see* Margaret.

And yet, Margaret was plainly missing.

"Tell her that I'm here," Jasper said.

Mr. Owens gritted his teeth. "I don't think that's wise."

"Of course it's bloody wise." Giving a woman a choice before she married the wrong man was a good thing. Anyone could see that. This didn't require any particular skills of perception, derived from ancestors who were witches or anything similarly ridiculous.

Jasper put his hands on his waist, but Mr. Owens only quirked an eyebrow. Most people found Jasper somewhat intimidating. No doubt Mr. Owens had heard too many stories to give him the requisite appreciation.

Mr. Owens glowered and rested his hands on his hips. "I want you far away from here."

"I'm not leaving."

Mr. Owens glowered. "You should."

"Not before I speak with Margaret."

Mr. Owens hurried quickly to the door, and Jasper followed him. Mr. Owens would show him where Margaret was. This was working. He would see her soon.

Mr. Owens nodded to the proprietor and jerked his thumb in Jasper's direction. "This man is following me."

"Oh?" The proprietor's bushy brows rose, and he pushed up his sleeves when he spotted Jasper.

"What are you doing?" the proprietor's wife asked.

"That's that ruffian who has been here all week. Claiming he was a duke. Most suspicious."

Blast.

The other patrons were listening to the conversation, and some narrowed their eyes and rose.

Jasper's heart beat at a quicker pace, and he leaped up and bolted up the stairs. Margaret was here. He just needed to find her.

"Margaret! Margaret!" he called, banging on doors of the guest rooms, conscious of people chasing him.

CHAPTER TWENTY-EIGHT

MARGARET PACED THE room. Tomorrow, she would become Mrs. Owens.

Her plan had worked. They were in Gretna Green, and tomorrow they would marry.

Except... Margaret wasn't the least bit happy.

Mr. Owens was gone. She could sneak away. Obviously, her reputation would be forever ruined, but...

Perhaps her father would agree for her to remain a spinster and not force the duke into an unwelcome, permanent union with her.

She hesitated, then opened the door tentatively to the corridor.

Commotion sounded from the corridor, then she spotted a man rushing toward the door. The man looked curiously like Jasper.

Obviously, she'd never be able to stop thinking of him, and she gave a wistful sigh.

"Margaret!" the man hollered. "Margaret!"

Her heartbeat quickened.

It couldn't be him.

She'd last seen him in Dorset.

And this was a posting inn in Scotland.

"Jasper?" she squeaked.

"Margaret!" the man rushed toward her. "You're here! I found you!"

"Er—yes." She stiffened. She resisted the urge to leap into his arms or any such sentimental nonsense. Instead, she eyed him cautiously.

Perhaps he desired to bring her back to the castle. No doubt her family had been shocked by her elopement. And perhaps he simply wanted to purchase something from the blacksmith's shop before they traveled back.

It was just that Gretna Green was *awfully* far Dorset.

Even the kindest host could hardly be expected to volunteer to return somebody to her parents after another guest absconded with her, no matter how much he concerned himself with his guests' every need.

No, there could be no other reason for him to be here. This was far from his castle.

He must have come for her.

Jasper might have stopped running, but voices and the sound of pounding feet still could be heard behind him.

People were chasing him? Margaret scrunched her eyebrows together.

"Blast it." Jasper turned to her. "You're coming with me."

"What?"

"Tell me you don't love that man," Jasper said.

"That's none of your business!"

"And that's not an answer." Jasper grinned and threw Margaret over his shoulder.

"What are you doing?" she shrieked.

"Carrying you," Jasper said. "I can carry things too."

Margaret didn't answer. The world was upside down. She was grateful the hotel proprietor had decided to decorate the inn with sideboards and potted plants, and not tables and porcelain vases. The walls looked sufficiently threatening, even if Jasper's grip was firm.

Jasper.

Margaret's heart pounded, and not simply for the excitement of being hauled away from her room.

He was here.

Truly here.

People appeared before her. Their faces were red, and they hollered vulgarities, most of which seemed to be about the importance of placing Margaret down.

"Where are we going?" she asked.

"To a certain blacksmith's shop!" Jasper shouted, while opening a door.

"A blacksmith's shop?" Margaret's heartbeat quickened.

Did Jasper mean—? She shook her head.

He couldn't mean *that*. She couldn't daydream he meant that. She simply couldn't allow herself to be disappointed.

They descended some stairs. People swarmed around them, and Jasper swore.

He set her down on her feet and clutched her hand. "Don't let go."

A tremor went through her at the touch of his warm hand. She hadn't had a chance to put on her gloves before leaving the room, and their skin touched, reminding her of their time in the maze.

"Hurry!" Jasper shouted, and they rushed through the crowd.

They exited the posting inn and onto the street. Jasper pulled her confidently along, and she soon spotted a blacksmith's shop.

Her heartbeat continued to quicken.

Jasper *did* seem very eager to go to the blacksmith's shop.

But then again, perhaps he'd broken a wheel to his coach and had found it vital to purchase a tool so he might fix it himself. Men could be quite attached to their carriages. Personally, Margaret would have hired someone with the tool in question, but then, no doubt there was a certain satisfaction in fixing the issue oneself.

But perhaps he didn't want to purchase anything.

Perhaps he—

She swallowed hard.

I won't hope. I won't hope. I won't hope.

They arrived at the blacksmith's shop. A queue of people was outside, but Jasper barged into the shop, still clutching her hand.

"You'll have to go in the back of the line," the blacksmith said.

"I'm the Duke of Jevington." Jasper let go of Margaret's hand, then he took out a small satchel that clinked in a most curious manner.

The blacksmith's eyes rounded, and he accepted it hastily.

"We've been waiting too!" A couple said behind. "You can't simply go ahead."

"The ceremony is short," the blacksmith said, as if worried Jasper might take the satchel back.

Jasper grinned and removed another satchel. He handed coins to everyone in the line, and gleeful murmurs sounded around Margaret.

Then he returned.

She stared at him, conscious she'd never met anyone like him, conscious her legs trembled, conscious everything might just be fine.

"What's happening?" she asked.

He grinned. "Did I not tell you? We're going to get married."

An orchestra began to play in her heart.

"You're proposing inside?" the blacksmith asked.

"Indeed." Jasper leaned closer to her. "So, what do you say, sweetheart?"

"But why?" she asked.

"Because I love you," he said, his voice more serious. "Because I adore you and want to spend the rest of my life with you. Because these past weeks without you have been appalling."

She was quiet.

"Now what do you say?" There was an odd pleading tone in his voice.

She struggled for breath. Emotions cascaded through her.

"Yes," she breathed.

Jasper swept her into his arms and kissed her.

"First things first," the blacksmith said sternly, and Margaret giggled.

A commotion sounded outside.

"Better be quick," Jasper said.

The blacksmith beamed. "That's my specialty."

JASPER WAS A MARRIED man and he led his bride into their bedroom.

A month ago, he would have thought the phrase would have struck fear in him, but a month ago, everything had been different. Now he was delighted. Ecstatic.

Music wafted from the public house below. He stared at Margaret. She was so lovely, so beautiful.

Jasper had refused to stay in Gretna Green, lest Mr. Owens cause more trouble. Still, Margaret and he were married, and there was little Mr. Owens could do. They'd returned back to the inn to fetch Juliet.

Margaret approached him. "You're grinning."

"I'm happy." He took her into his arms and kissed her.

The kiss was long and delicious, and he clutched her to him.

"I love you," he said.

"I love you too."

Jasper stroked her hair. The bed might not be as sumptuous as the beds in his various properties, but he'd never been so eager to be in one. He flung her onto it. Removing clothes had never been so important, and he wished he hadn't delegated so much of his clothes removing process to his valet. Any advantage would be valuable now.

Because Jasper's skin needed to be against Margaret's skin.

He craved her, as he'd never craved anyone before.

His manhood grew, ready to plunge into her, ready to immerse himself in Margaret's softness, Margaret's warmth, Margaret's wonderfulness.

Her eyes were wide, as if still incredulous at his presence. He despised that.

He abhorred that anyone had ever made Margaret feel dismissed. He vowed to make Margaret feel magnificent.

Because she *was* magnificent.

He kissed her throat. It wasn't his first time kissing her throat, and it wouldn't be his last.

She shuddered against him, clasping onto his shirt, as if she thought she might faint. Her vanilla scent wafted over him.

He needed more.

More soft flesh to kiss, more silky locks to delve his hands into, more *Margaret*.

He turned her over and fiddled with her stays until they were sufficiently loosened.

This was Margaret's back.

And this was Margaret's right shoulder. And this was Margaret's left shoulder.

Everything about Margaret was perfect.

"I thought I'd lost you," Jasper groaned.

"I'm here now."

"Oh, yes you bloody are." Jasper continued to kiss her. Deeply, desperately. Because he needed to ascertain that she wasn't simply an apparition, that she was truly here, truly his.

He'd dreamed of this moment for days, and he didn't want to wake up in some posting inn and know he'd only conjured her.

"We're married," Margaret murmured. "I'm not going anywhere."

"Say it again," Jasper said.

"We're married. And I'm not going anywhere."

Jasper thrust more quickly inside her, allowing the words to sweep through him.

They were married.

And she wasn't going to leave again.

And they were going to live happily-ever-after.

EPILOGUE

SEVEN WEEKS LATER

The carriage halted before Margaret's parents' townhouse.

Jasper extended his hand to Margaret. "Ready?"

She nodded and exited the coach. Her legs moved stiffly after the long carriage ride. They'd taken their time returning from Scotland, driving Juliet to her home in Northumberland, then stopping in picturesque villages and admiring the idyllic countryside.

She quelled her sudden nervousness and strode toward her former home. The black wrought iron gate gleamed in the familiar manner, as did the white walls. She glanced at Jasper, then grasped hold of the door knocker.

The butler opened the door immediately and ushered her inside. She stepped over the familiar marble flooring.

This time though, everything was different.

This time she was married.

"Ah! Miss Carberry—I mean, Your Grace!" the butler sputtered, even though normally his expression only changed when his lips twitched after one of her parents or her used a particularly Scottish word.

"Good afternoon, Jameson."

257

Jasper followed her into the foyer, and the butler's eyes goggled.

"And Your Grace!" Jameson swept into a sudden bow.

Even though Margaret had never known Jameson to not emulate calmness, his voice seemed decidedly more halting and his cheeks seemed a distinct rosier shade.

"Mrs. Carberry is in the drawing room," the butler said. "She'll be delighted to see you."

"Thank you." Margaret turned to Jasper. "It's just to the right."

Footsteps sounded, then her mother barreled toward them, a flurry of carmine cotton. Her cap swayed on her head, and she pushed it up. "Dearest! You're back!"

"Yes," Margaret squeaked.

"Margaret, you should have told me you were coming. And you've brought the *duke*." Mama's voice reached a high-pitched squeak, as if she were assisting someone tune the loftiest notes of a piano.

Mama looked around frantically, then hollered for a maid. "Cecelia! We must have tea! We cannot have a duke here and not offer him tea. What will the man think of us?"

"I'll inform the housekeeper," Cecelia said.

"At once," Mama said. "You must run!"

Cecelia's face whitened, but she dutifully sprinted down the glossy corridor, managing to slide only twice before she disappeared through the door to the stairs.

"Oh, my dear duke!" Mama clasped her hands together. "There will be tea. If you can be patient—"

"Mrs. Carberry," Jasper said. "We are family now."

"Family!" Mama staggered back, and her eyes glimmered. "So we are." She glanced at Grandmother Agatha. "What do you think of that?"

"I think it's lovely," Grandmother Agatha declared, before kissing their cheeks.

Margaret's mother leaned toward him. "You *must* call me Mama."

Jasper's chin wobbled. "Perhaps we can stick with Mrs. Carberry."

Mama tossed him a coy smile. "For now." She dashed toward the library and pounded on the thick oak door. "Mr. Carberry! We have a guest! An important one."

"Two guests," Jasper said.

Mama's eyes widened, then her gaze dropped to Margaret and she grinned. "My dear duke. You are good at counting. Such talent!" She pounded on the door again. "Mr. Carberry!"

Her voice soared through the townhouse. If Mama's voice were less grating, she could have enjoyed a career as an opera singer.

Papa appeared, clutching a folder. He straightened immediately. "My dear daughter! And—"

"Your new son," Mama declared proudly.

"Er—yes." Papa approached Jasper. "We were delighted to receive your letter. Absolutely elated. You have my strongest congratulations."

Mama clapped her hands together, and the ribbons on her cap wobbled. "I did it! I arranged this!"

Margaret sighed. "That's not true."

But Mama's smile remained on her face. She clasped her hands together, and even though Margaret had never known her mother to be prone to jumping, unless to avoid a particularly egregious puddle, this time she did.

"I'm so happy!" Mama breathed.

Margaret glanced at Jasper.

He squeezed her hand. "I'm happy as well."

"My dear," Mama said. "I don't know why you gave me a difficult time earlier. Just think of the extra weeks of happiness I could have bestowed you if you'd allowed yourself to be discovered in a compromising position."

"Mama," Margaret said sternly.

Jasper's lips twitched. "She might have a point, Maggie."

"Nonsense. She mustn't be encouraged. Would you want her to do something similar to our child? She may have time to improve her knot-tying skills."

Jasper whitened. "No, no. That's unnecessary."

Mama's eyes glimmered. "What made you mention a child, dear?"

Fiddle-faddle.

The room suddenly warmed.

"Please tell me you're expecting," Mama continued.

Margaret swallowed hard, but she refused to lie.

Not about this.

Jasper turned his head and stared. "You don't mean that—"

Margaret nodded, and Jasper beamed.

The housekeeper and Cecelia appeared with tea, but Jasper took her in his arms and spun her around, even though her parents were present, even though servants were present.

"I'm so very happy," he said finally, his voice oddly hoarse.

"I am as well."

And she was.

MY FAVORITE DUKE

LADY JULIET IS HAPPY. *Very* happy. After all, she's engaged, even if she rarely sees her betrothed. So what if her betrothed keeps postponing their wedding? Or that there are wicked rumors about him? Still, when the Duke of Sherwood doesn't appear at a ball as intended, there's only one thing she can do: discover the truth herself.

Lucas, the Duke of Ainsworth, is exceedingly dull.

At least, that's what he desires everyone to believe. He makes certain to enter into conversations with the *ton* about obscure plants and to quote Latin tomes while fiddling with his spectacles. By night, Lucas is involved in a different task: bringing down criminals.

No criminal is as elusive as the person spreading counterfeit coin through the Lake District, and Lucas is determined to discover the source. When he sees someone sneak onto the man's estate in the Lake District, he expects to discover one of the man's accomplices. Instead, he is shocked to discover Lady Juliet. Lucas vows to help her, no matter how distracting her alluring presence is.

261

MORE BOOKS BY BIANCA BLYTHE

The Duke Hunters Club

When they were in finishing school, they vowed to marry dukes. Now, after their first season, they realize that plan might be impossible. Or is it?

All You Need is a Duke

My Favorite Duke

A Duke Never Forgets

Wedding Trouble

Shy bluestockings aren't supposed to marry dukes. When one dashing Scottish duke is determined to defy convention, everything changes. Curl up with this entertaining and charming series!

Don't Tie the Knot

Dukes Prefer Bluestockings

The Earl's Christmas Consultant

How to Train a Viscount

The Bachelor Marquess

A Holiday Proposal

Matchmaking for Wallflowers

Immerse yourself in these fun, light-hearted novels set in Regency England, filled with handsome rogues, feisty heroines, and adventure!

How to Capture a Duke

A Rogue to Avoid

Runaway Wallflower

Mad About the Baron

To Catch a Baroness

The Wrong Heiress for Christmas

Do you know that Bianca also writes cozy historical mysteries as Camilla Blythe? Click below to check them out.

Calamity under the Chandelier

Danger on the Downs

The Body in Bloomsbury

A Continental Murder

MEET THE AUTHOR

BORN IN TEXAS, BIANCA Blythe spent four years in England. She worked in a fifteenth-century castle, though sadly that didn't actually involve spotting dukes and earls strutting about in Hessians.

She credits British weather for forcing her into a library, where she discovered her first Julia Quinn novel. Thank goodness for blustery downpours.

Bianca now lives in California with her husband.

CONNECT WITH BIANCA

Chat with Bianca and other like-minded readers as well as learn about new books and giveaways as soon as they happen! Come join Bianca's VIP FB reader group.
https://www.facebook.com/groups/biancablythereaders
Or perhaps you'd like to sign up for Bianca's newsletter and receive an exclusive short story, Lord Perfect, along with new release alerts, giveaways, and updates!
join.biancablythe.com

Made in the USA
Columbia, SC
09 March 2021

34099633R00162